PETROV'S ESCAPE

WM. HOVEY SMITH

Petrov's Escape

WM. HOVEY SMITH

ISBN: 978-1-967375-92-9 (Paperback)

ISBN: 978-1-967375-93-6 (E-book)

Library of Congress Control Number: 2025921199

Printed in the United States of America

Published by:

info@thequippyquill.com
(302) 295-2278

Contents

CHAPTER 1
PETROV'S ESCAPE

The frigid blast of an early winter storm was beating against the walls of the forge as Petrov and his father were pounding out a long shaft to put on a canoe to let it navigate the shallow drainages of the Bureya River. Soon, even the larger Amur would freeze, and Shaka would be cut off from the world except for emergency helicopter flights.

"Dad, I've got to leave. Now. They got Ivan yesterday. They just grabbed him off the street and told him he was going into the Army. No warning. No goodbyes. No nothing. They just took him." Petrov said, pausing to see if his words had any effect on his stoic dad. Ankarov had been in Stalin's prisons and exiled to this isolated Siberian village. He had seen much and lived much, and nothing about the workings of the present Russian Federation surprised or interested him. He just wanted to be here with his son and live his life.

Seeing no response, Petrov continued more vigorously. "I think Putin is wrong in what he is trying to do in Ukraine. I don't want any part in it. If Russia were facing a real enemy, I would gladly go, but not for this."

"I need you here. The village needs you. You are a skilled forger, a machinist, and can fix anything. I'll argue against them taking you," Ankarov replied.

A banging on the door interrupted their conversation.

"Open up. This is Commissar Robisky. I want to see your son."

"I'm forging, give me a second, please," Ankarov replied. Without breaking the rhythm of his hammering, Ankarov whispered to his son," Take your tools and get into the basement quickly."

Petrov pulled open the trap door in the floor, threw his tongs down into the basement, climbed down, and pulled the door shut. As soon as he was in, Ankarov scattered coal over the floor and pulled a wooden box over the door. The pounding became more insistent.

"I'm coming. I'm coming," Ankarov shouted.

When he opened the door, he saw the Commissar dressed in a wolf fur coat and two guards dressed in winter whites carrying SKS rifles slung over their shoulders. The three entered the forge along with a fresh blast of snow, which melted as soon as it hit.

"Where is your son?" Robisky demanded as he pulled out a notebook and looked at a list of names. "Where is Petrov?"

"I'm sorry. I don't know. I sent him to town, and he has not returned," Ankarov informed.

"We'll wait. It's warm here. Please continue what you were doing. I like to see men moving metal. You men take off your coats, turn that box over, and have a seat. We will spend a little time here," Robisky ordered as he took off his coat and shook the snow from the fur, revealing a somewhat portly man compared to his younger, less well-fed companions. One was tall, broad across the shoulders, while the other was shorter and thinner to the extent that he looked like he should still be in secondary school.

Petrov cringed as he heard the box being drug on the floor above him, flipped, and the men's shoes shuffling on the floor as they sat. Somehow, he had to get out tonight. He knew that if he left, he could never come back. Dissenters and evaders could be turned in by school children or anyone else. Only the frozen vastness of the Siberian wilderness offered refuge.

Ankarov put more coal and turned on the bellows to make it uncomfortably hot in the small forge. He worked to make a second shaft, although he did not need the part.

"The Federation wants men like your son who grew up in these small villages because they know how to live in the cold and do real work, unlike their soft city cousins who are accountants and store clerks. Petrov has been reported to have supported the opposition and spoken out against our leaders and even quoted passages from banned books.

If he does not volunteer to do his patriotic duty, he will be put in an assault brigade and likely have the honor of dying for The Motherland," Robisky informed in a commanding tone.

"My son has perhaps been somewhat rash in expressing his opinions, but he has a vital set of forging and mechanical skills that are more important to the village than politics or going away to fight in a war thousands of kilometers away," Ankarov argued.

"That is exactly why The State wants him and will have him. He will be an asset on the battlefield and would possibly be assigned to a support facility and not a combat unit. We also need men to keep our equipment running," Robisky said with his voice starting to show irritation by being prodded into stating the obvious.

Heat was starting to build inside the forge, and as the Commissar and his men were starting to sweat in their clothing, he motioned for them to dress.

"It will go hard for you if Petrov does not turn himself in or you attempt to hide him. Remember that. You will go back to prison and lose everything you have. I have warned you and will not do so again." With these stern words, the Commissar and his men left.

"You were right. You must leave tonight. Take our boat and make your way downriver to that trapper's cabin we found. Take whatever food is in the house and our traps and snares. Stay out all winter. I'll get the Amurisky ready and put all the fuel we have into it. No time for goodbyes. Take this gold cross of your mother's, get your shit together, and go," Ankarov ordered as he took the cross and chain off his neck and thrust it into his son's hands.

With a bag full of supplies from the house, Petrov rejoined his father in the forge when the door burst open and the two soldiers rushed into the room and lowered their guns on Ankarov and Petrov.

Ankarov took a shovel of burning coal from the forge and threw it into the face of one of the troopers who fired his gun. The bullet ripped through Ankarov's chest, expelling blood and bone from his back. As the Commissar attempted to draw his pistol, Petrov grabbed the other trooper's SKS, turned it on the three men, and kept shooting until they quit moving. Throwing the gun down, he rushed to the aid of his father, who was gasping for breath and spitting frothy blood from his mouth.

Taking his father's head in his hands, he said, "I'm sorry. I'm sorry. What should I do?"

"Take what money and things you can use from the house and these men, set fire to everything, and leave," he said as he made a final struggle to speak. Apparently satisfied that his message had been received, he pushed against his son's arms and whispered, "Go. Let me die. Go."

Tears streamed down Petrov's face as he laid his father's head down as gently as possible and watched as Ankarov convulsed in a coughing fit and died. Wiping his tears with a shop rag, he recovered money from the Commissar's billfold, took his fur coat and watch, the internal passport from the trooper who looked most like him, and the small amount of money they had. He took the winter over-whites and winter trousers from one of the bodies and pulled the three men over the pile of coal in the storage stall.

Going back to the house, he took as much canned food, salt, sugar, and flour as he could fit into the canoe, and before he shut the door of the only home he had ever known, he used kerosene to start a fire in an interior room. Time was short. He had to set fire to the forge and launch before the villagers noticed.

Pausing for only a few seconds before what was to become the funeral pyre for his father, the Commissar, and the two men. He prayed, "Dear God, please take my father and these men into thy heavenly grace and forgive me for what I have done. May it be pleasing to you to help us all in this time of strife."

With these words, he ignited the coal and went through the blizzard down to the landing, polled the canoe into deeper water, and pulled on the cord to start the 30-hp Whirlwind outboard engine. Only half the starter cord was pulled out as the wet grip slipped from his cold fingers. The second time, the recoil starter functioned, although it was a very hard pull as the grease had nearly solidified in the cold. The third and fourth times, the pulls became smoother. On the fifth attempt, the engine sputtered.

His dad had always joked that he thought that outboard engines were "Instruments of the Devil, sent to beset mankind."

This unwanted thought was not welcomed as he pulled again and got a sputter and a wheeze.

"Come on, old fellow, you do it. We will have adventures. I'll take you to waters that you have never seen," he promised.

Crossing himself to gain favor from all sources, he pulled again. There was a sputter, a blast with an issue of black smoke out of the tailpipe, and slowly a ka-whomp, ka-whomp, ka-whomp, as the engine started to turn up to an idle speed. He dipped the prop deeper into the water as the boat started to move forward, and a stream of water came from the exhaust port. Only then did he stand fully upright and twist the throttle to provide propulsion against the water and blizzard winds. As they headed downriver towards an unknown future, the sky behind him was reddening from the burning buildings, and he could hear the alarm bell from the village church.

For the first time in his life, he was alone, completely and utterly alone. He had to concentrate on what he was doing as the force of the Bureya River's currents and the blowing blizzard threatened to take control of his craft and drive him into the bank or into the clutches of washed-in trees, which threatened to rise from the river and swat him like a fly.

When he could no longer see to make safe headway, he went into a quiet oxbow, breaking through the skim ice to land on a sandy bar somewhat protected against the storm. He huddled in the back of the boat, wrapped in the Commissar's coat, and pulled whatever clothing he could lay his hands on around him so he was bundled like a Peruvian mummy. In the morning, he ate cold canned fish and three tablespoons of sugar and pushed off again. He hoped that anyone investigating the fire would assume that one of those bodies was his, which might buy him a little time.

He pushed hard to get as far downriver as he could. The continuing storm was suppressing ordinary fishing and boating traffic, and what houses he passed were tightly shuttered. The river freighter and barge that he passed were anchored in quieter water. With the roar of the wind, few, if any, would hear his boat's motor or see his small craft on the water. The storm was aiding his escape.

He ran the Amurisky standing in the back of the craft, which caused his legs and arms to cramp under the strain of controlling the boat and fighting the wind, although he could get a small amount of rest when he was under the lee of a tall bank. He was trying hard to remember every feature of the river because it would be easy to miss the small tributary stream where the cabin was located.

In Soviet times, single men would be assigned trapping areas where they would Trap all Winter and bring their furs to the collective to sell in the Spring. Their returns for the fur were often not enough to pay the amount owed for supplies, so with an admonition to work harder, they were sent back to prepare for the next season after any medical and social needs were met. Thousands of these cabins were built throughout the vastness of Siberia, with most being abandoned with the fall of the Soviet Union, as many of the trappers sought easier lives in metropolitan areas or emigrated. With this general depopulation, the Bureya Nature Reserve was established in 1987.

"What I am doing is probably illegal, but compared to triple homicide, what difference would it make?" he thought as he laughed out loud. Dark humor it was, but it was welcomed. That was the first bit of levity he had felt since his father's death, and he started to feel a little bit like his old self again.

Petrov was looking for a bold bluff of black stone because he knew that the stream that he and his father had found was about half a kilometer further down the river on the opposite side. It was with a great sense of relief that he spotted the stream junction and turned his canoe into it. It was deeper here, but he knew that it quickly shallowed, and he would have to keep his propeller from striking any of the large rocks or boulders that had been dragged down By glaciers along with gold which could sometimes be found in economic amounts among the boulders. If one were persistent, a few colors could be panned from almost any stream, as he and his father had done.

He felt as if a burden had been lifted off his shoulders when he spotted the cabin. It was made of sturdy logs half-dug into the hillside and covered with a roof of tarpaper and sod. There was one glass window that let in some light. Before he beached his boat, he looked carefully to see if anyone was there. No smoke was coming from the central chimney, and broken branches were half hanging from the roof. Getting out of the boat, he walked over to the cabin door, lifted the heavy latching bar, and pushed. The door had apparently settled a bit, but as he applied pressure to the thick door of hand-split planks, it opened enough for him to thrust his head inside. Everything was intact. There was a steel box stove in the middle of the room, a bunk bed, a table, and chairs that were all made of poles and timbers from the surrounding forests. There were also traps and snares hung from the walls, blankets, pots, knives, a good broad-bladed ax, and even Chinese porcelain dishes. There were also two kerosene lanterns and books. The dry climate had preserved everything, and even the pages of the books looked like new.

"This guy was a dissident," Petrov remarked as he looked through a selection of bound books, handwritten manuscripts, and printed-off copies held in loose-leaf binders. Among the titles were "Doctor Zhivago" by Boris Pasternak, 1984 by George Orwell, "One Day in the Life of Ivan Denisovich" by Aleksandr Solzhenitsyn, and "We" by Yevgeny Zamyatin. His father had told him about some of these books, but he had never seen them. In Soviet times, a person could even be imprisoned for possessing such a book, so they had stayed in this cabin perhaps for him to discover.

On the dust-covered base of the lamp was a rendition of a Chinese scholar. He felt an impulse to kiss the spider web and dust-covered lamp out of reverence to his unknown benefactor, but that would wait until he cleaned everything up and settled in.

"Is this what I am supposed to do to redeem myself?" he wondered. Petrov found himself saying a silent prayer of thanks to his unknown benefactor and to the others he had killed, including the two soldiers who were not so different from himself.

"How am I so much better than them that they should die, and he should live?" he questioned. "They wanted lives, family, children, and everything else, too. And his dad had sacrificed himself to let him get away. I am no hero. Am I really, in my true heart, a self-absorbed coward?"

******

Using the snowshoes at the cabin, he cut a trail and set traps for marmot, mink, otter, beaver, and wolverine. He used the snares for snowshoe rabbits and wolves. He was thankful that the bears had gone into hibernation and had left the cabin alone. He did not enjoy killing anything, but he needed to raise money for his escape and take animals for food. Beavers had been reintroduced by the Soviets in the 1960s and had regained their position in the ecosystem by stabilizing wetlands and providing habitat for a variety of species.

In an ironic twist, Petrov thought, "Even bad governments can do some good. It's a pity that they care more for their animals than their people."

Later in the season, while walking at the base of a steep bank on a creek, he noticed a sharply tapered root sticking out of the snow. The next time he passed, the snow had been mostly blown away, and that section of the creek bed was bare. He realized that what he had been looking at was not a wind-polished root, but a mammoth tusk. Excitedly, he went back to the cabin and brought his ax and a grubbing hoe to dig it out. It was two meters long and ten centimeters across the base. It was covered with a dark rime which protected the solid white ivory beneath. He would have to return with a harness to drag it home. That tusk could be traded for whatever he needed on the black market in any town close to the Chinese border.

Although it was going to be a long, cold winter alone with his doubts and fears, that chance find brought him hope.

CHAPTER 2

THE LONG WINTER

A month later, Petrov awoke to a crackling sound and the feeling that his hair was being electrified. Looking out the window, he could see the dancing northern lights more clearly than he had ever seen them in Shaka. He threw off the reindeer hide he had been sleeping under and put his socked feet into his boots. As he passed the stove, he added a couple of blocks of wood.

When he stepped outside, blue, green, red, and purple sheets danced and seemed to fold and unfold across the sky. His Nanai friends told him that these lights were the spirits of the dead trying to find their way. The worst was if the lights turned red; they were vengeful, and some misfortune would likely fall on those who saw them, particularly if the lights came down toward the earth. As he watched, a red curtain split into three parts and violently darted through the sky, as if searching.

Petrov fell to his knees and prayed, "Please, dear Mother Mary and all the saints, protect me. Yes. I have killed, because I did not want to take part in killing others. Of this I am guilty. Punish me if you like, but let my life be of some greater help to mankind so that their lives and my life will not have been spent in vain. Intercede with your Holy Son and help me in my hour of trial."

Unable to watch at least some even more deadly sign be revealed, he sat on his bunk, put his head in his hands, and wept. The image that troubled him most was of the teenager who had held his hands up in a plea for mercy as he pumped the last bullets into him. "As I showed no mercy, can I expect any?" he asked himself. There was no answer as he fell into a troubled sleep, as the sounds of a howling pack of wolves entered his dream world.

He saw himself injured and pursued by a running pack of wolves as he fled, trailing drops of blood on the snow. The lead wolf, an old male, gained on him with every step. Crossing a frozen creek, he could feel the ice cracking beneath his feet. As he clawed his way up the bank towards the forest, he saw the large gray wolf 50 meters behind him. More frantic now, he ran through the trees until his foot caught on a branch under the snow, and he fell. Backing up against a tree, he drew his Makarov pistol and waited. He could go no further.

The big wolf came, bared his teeth, and snarled. Its silver hairs bristled from its back as it started to provide its pack with their next meal. Sinking back on its haunches, the wolf prepared for its final assault. Petrov cocked the pistol and pulled the trigger. The hammer fell on an empty chamber. As he attempted to rack the slide with his gloved hands, the magazine fell into the snow. He drew his knife and made ready for the end.

He knew what would happen. The alpha wolf would rip his throat with his teeth and use the claws on his rear feet to open his stomach and pull out his intestines. Then the rest of the pack would pile on him to feed while he was still alive. That was the way of the wolf, and he knew it. Soaked with sweat, Petrov awoke and cried out.

Although this dream had spared him from witnessing his own death, he expected that it was a sign of impending doom. He stoked up the stove and cooked himself some frozen rabbit meat, cattails, and wild onions with a hunk of fat from a young beaver. He took salty dirt from the cabin floor, dissolved the salt out of it with water, strained any floating particles out with a cloth, and added the water to the pot.

As the cabin warmed, he took off the sweaty clothes and hung them out to dry. It gave him little comfort that the dry clothes that he put on had been taken from the larger of the two guardsmen that he had killed. After he arrived, he had washed out most of the blood and patched four bullet holes.

"I'm an easy mark wearing these clothes. I know it. If you bastards want me, I'm here. I'm sorry, you have every right to come after me. I know. I know that. Whatever fate awaits me, I'm ready," Petrov told the spirits.

Whenever the weather allowed, he had to check his five kilometers of traplines. Trudging through the snow, he had beaten paths that he could follow even after fresh snowfalls. Each time he went, he would attempt to remove any obstacles so that he could more easily drag a sled down the trail. This proved particularly handy when he spotted a moose in a tributary valley while he was gathering willow wands to use to build stretch-frames for his hides. Retiring as quietly as he could, he went to the cabin, grabbed one of the SKS rifles, and returned. The moose had moved, but he followed its tracks a few hundred meters to where it was still browsing.

Stealthfully, he approached. With the military cartridges, he had to hit the spine or brain to drop it where it stood. A body shot might kill the large cow, but it might run for days before it died. Even in the over whites, 30 meters was as close as he dared approach. As quietly as he could, he pulled the safety back. Then he flipped the cover off the trigger finger and felt the wool glove liner pull on the trigger. It began its long travel before it tripped the sear, and the gun would fire. He knew he had to be patient. As his father always warned, a jerk on the trigger could cause him to wound the animal.

Although only seconds, it seemed longer before the gun fired. Snow blew off the surrounding willows, but the bullet flew true. The moose collapsed. It attempted to raise its head, and its legs thrashed before Petrov could shoot it in its head. Whenever he had been involved in a moose hunt, there had always been others to help because a single quarter could weigh between 50 and 100 kilos. He was nearly a kilometer from his cabin. He did not skin the animal but took his ax and chopped out the rear leg. He would take the front leg on that side on the next trip. When he came back, he would extract the backstraps and neck. Only then would he be able to turn the animal over.

As more hide and meat were taken off the animal, the carcass would attract crows, jays, and ravens, who would announce the kill to the world. Any nearby wolves and smaller carnivores would be attracted to the carcass, but thankfully, no bears, or so Petrov hoped. He had an embarrassment of riches if he could get as much of that moose home to the cabin and keep it safe. He felt satisfied three days later when he had salvaged about two-thirds of the meat, including some tasty liver which he would consume as a partial preventive of scurvy as he was having increasing difficulty in chopping roots out of the rock-hard ground or finding berries beneath the snow to provide vitamin C. Without dental care he did not want to lose teeth or have his bones soften.

A few days after he killed the moose, he left the cabin at the first glimmer of daylight with the sun hanging low in the southern horizon as it made its slow arc across the sky. He checked his martin and mink traps first in the spruce trees that grew along the stream banks. Looking up, he saw that he had caught a martin in his trap set in a bent-over tree. He recovered the frozen martin and reset the trap, baiting it with a frozen red squirrel, the animal's favorite food.

His next trap was set for mink, who preferred fish for bait. This one was empty, so he passed by without touching it. Further up the stream, he approached the remains of the moose. On his last meat haul, he had set snares on a trail of wolf tracks. He drew his pistol when he heard the sound of an animal thrashing to pull the heavy log on the other end of the snare. The main part of the snare was around the "volchitsa's" neck. This was not the gray wolf of his dreams, but an adult female. As Petrov approached, it turned and lunged at him, momentarily cutting off its air supply. Petrov carefully placed one shot through its ear into its brain. It fell kicking and finally lay quiet.

Petrov stopped and stroked the animal on its back. "Old momma wolf, today I will feed on you and take comfort from your fur. Tomorrow, your pups may feed on me. Such is the way of the world. Peace be to you and yours."

He dared not leave this valuable animal least other wolves or more likely a wolverine would find it and damage the fur. He carefully opened the animal and removed the guts, keeping the heart and liver to use as bait in some of his other traps. Once he got the animal to the cabin, he would skin it while it still retained some body heat and make a frame to hold it. Every bit of flesh needed to be removed before the hide could be washed in salt water, dried, scraped, and salted. After salting, it was scraped again, and oil was added to make it subtle. There was curing oil at the cabin, and he recovered more from boiling the animal's brains.

This was slow, meticulous work, but he was glad for it. These tasks gave him something productive to do to help pass the dark days and nights of a Siberian winter. When he wanted a change from processing fur, he worked on finishing a pair of ivory grips for his pistol and building traps. When he finished something significant, he rewarded himself by reading some chapters of the books that his benefactor had left behind.

******

One of the few bonding moments that he and Ankarov ever had was building radios from parts salvaged from broken ones that they tuned to receive the Voice of America broadcast from Alaska. They removed the motherboards and tubes and concealed them in larger pieces of furniture, like the backs of chests of drawers, and left only the headphone jack exposed in one of the drawers. To a passerby, a person would be seen reading a book while listening to music on their headphones.

He had helped Ankarov put these together. Petrov had hurriedly packed radio parts in his Amurisky as he left, but he was only partly successful in getting the radio working at the cabin because of the limited amount of energy that the solar cells could supply during the fleeting daylight hours when he would be trapping or fishing.

Petrov felt pride when he learned about Russia's early space successes in school and was puzzled why Americans seemed to broadcast everything, including disasters such as rockets blowing up on the launch pad and the Challenger disaster a few years after he was born. He was reminded of Lenin's quote, "Knowledge is a dangerous thing, that is why we control it so fiercely."

"Could it really be that way in America?" he asked.

Ankarov had responded with a noncommittal, "The Americans would like us to think so."

******

Days grew longer as Spring approached. At times, water would drip from the spruce and fir trees, and masses of snow caught in the branches would loosen and fall with a dull thud. Welcoming Spring was done at the village with a festival, drinking, dancing, and singing. Petrov felt a primal need to celebrate in whatever way he could. There were still blueberries on the frozen branches of the bushes. He gathered a pail full and brought them inside to ferment. After they warmed, he crushed them and added honey, and covered the pail with a cloth to keep the flies out while the natural yeast started to produce alcohol. He could distill this liquid with a still made from a combination of pots and copper fuel lines that his predecessor had accumulated. The potatoes he had brought from the house were long gone. Although this would not be vodka, it would be something. Through the coiled copper tube came the drip, drip, drip of clear liquid. He caught a bit of it on his finger and put it on his tongue. "Yes. I have brandy!" he exclaimed. "Brandy. Real brandy."

With the smell of alcohol in the air and a slow drip from the coil, Petrov became increasingly impatient, "Damn. It's taking forever. Hurry up. Will you hurry up?" he shouted.

Sitting back in his homemade chair, he closed his eyes and thought about the last Spring Festival at the village when he had appeared in his best clothes in hopes of attracting the eye of the baker's daughter, Louisa, who was scheduled to go to University. With his broad shoulders, tanned skin, muscled torso, and stature was even in his own eyes, a manly figure. Now outfitted in his finest, "How could she possibly resist," he thought.

He was stuck in the village because his father's exile prevented him from going to the University despite having done as well as she had on his exams. "Maybe, even if only for one night, they could be together," he thought. He remembered that he had two condoms in his billfold just in case that Ivan had given to him.

They had danced. They laughed. They drank. Finally, Petrov got up enough vodka courage to ask, "Louisa, we may never see each other again. You are going to start a new life that I cannot be part of. I want, very much, for us to be together even if it is only once. I have loved you all through school, and this may be our last night. Will you…"

"Yes. Yes. Yes." She enthusiastically replied. "I thought you would never get around to asking. I'd seen you in the sauna. I've wanted you to be my first."

"Me too," Petrov answered with a blush running across his face.

"Let's go to my house. No one is home," Louisa responded.

"Your dad will kill me," Petrov replied.

"No, he won't. He gave me some condoms in case I brought someone home. He likes you. He said so," Louisa assured her bed-partner-to-be.

"You mean," Petrov stammered.

"Yes, I mean," Louisa assured as she grabbed Petrov by the hand and half-dragged him out of the crowd and down the street to the bakery.

Opening the door with her key, she led Petrov up the stairs to an apartment. Quickly passing through the living and dining rooms, she flung open her bedroom door, pushed Petrov in, and turned the key in the lock.

"What?" Petrov asked.

"Shut up," Louisa responded. She turned to him, kissed him on the lips, and ran her tongue inside his mouth as her fingers unbuttoned his jacket and started to pull it off his shoulders.

"Get those things off," she demanded as she stepped back and started undoing her top before stepping out of her dress. Now, in only their underwear, they were face-to-face.

Slowly rolling up his undershirt, she paused at his erect nipples and kissed them as she pulled the shirt off his arms and ran her fingers over his ribs to return and circle around the nipples.

"Now you," she ordered.

Petrov reached behind Louisa's back and unsnapped the bra and watched as the fleshy globes of her breasts fell. Then he repeated Louisa's gestures with his hands as his rising erection became more apparent, as it strained against his underwear.

Louisa bent and pushed the elastic waistband down over Petrov's hips, revealing first the head and then the shaft of his manhood as it pointed towards his navel.

Without waiting for instructions, Petrov slid off Louisa's panties and viewed the bushy forest of pubic hair that concealed the opening that his penis was straining to penetrate.

"To bed," Louisa barked like a Marine Sergeant as she threw back the covers, reached into a bedside table, and drew out a condom packet, which she cut with scissors and withdrew the latex device.

Like her dad showed her with a zucchini, she placed it on Petrov's shaft and then mounted him like a jockey about to give him the ride of his life. To the sweet smell of cinnamon, nutmeg, and baking bread,

Petrov had his first sexual encounter. He tried not to come too quickly, but years of pent-up passion would not be denied. It gushed as he moaned with pleasure. His head had been stiffly raised, but now fell back on the pillow. Still with his shaft inside her, Louisa bent over and kissed him. "It's all right. You're on top next time."

There had been a next time, and a next time, and a next time as they explored the sexual possibilities offered by their bodies to the smells of ancient spices and music from the villagers outside.

A sizzle from the blueberry mash pot brought Petrov out of his memories. He should have stopped the process earlier, but even having the smell of alcohol had brought such sweet memories that he did not feel disappointed with the results.

Carefully taking the half liter of product he had captured, he poured it into a cup and set it outside to cool in a mound of snow. After it chilled, he brought it back inside and toasted, "To Louisa, to Spring, and a better world tomorrow than we have today."

CHAPTER 3
TIMELY FRIENDS

As well situated as Petrov had made himself in the cabin, it was time to leave. The ice had mostly broken up on his stream, and he had to consider what he could take to continue his journey to Ukraine. He had to take his tusk, tarps, food, clothes, his furs, plus all the fuel cans. He would also have to stop for supplies, where he would have to present some identification.

Retaining the identification papers of the soldier that he most closely resembled, he carefully sorted through everything that he had brought and found in the cabin. He must leave no trace. Although this was a nature reserve, there were hikers, hippies, prospectors, and naturalists who roamed the area during the Summer and would report the presence of a wanted murderer. He would leave the cabin as much as possible as he found it.

With reluctance and deep regret, he burned the books that had given him so much comfort during the winter and only kept the bible. He took a single cooking pot, made up a metal tripod for suspending it over a fire, some pieces of hard flint and steel for starting fires, along with punky rotten wood and solidified tree rosin, which he sealed in a tin box.

The Amurisky needed attention. Drying over the winter, it had developed cracks which he had to patch with birch resin made from boiling the bark of the trees. This glue would set into a hard, flexible repair. For good measure, he overlayed it with pitch derived from hunks of sticky sap gathered from scarred spruce trees.

He didn't have much fuel left. He knew he would have to buy some before he tackled the Amur. If his fuel ran out, he could not steer the boat and could easily be run down by much larger river boats or even be sunk by a hunk of river ice.

He had about 10,000 rubles from what he took from his home and the men he had killed. If he did not have to sell his furs or ivory, perhaps he would not have to prove his identity. He hoped that he could pass as one of the Old Believer's sons who had spent a winter trapping. The Believers had fled to the Siberian wilderness centuries ago to practice what they thought was the truest and best version of the Russian Orthodox faith and had been in Siberia ever since.

******

Satisfied that he had a plan, he turned the boat upright, put rollers he had made from cut limbs under the canoe, closed the cabin door for the last time, and pushed off into the stream that, like twigs on a tree, would take him to the Bureya and then to the Amur. He would stop at one of the smaller trading posts, where he would be less likely to have to undergo official inspection and have his ivory or furs taken under some semi-official pretext or even be arrested. He hoped that with his long hair and beard, he looked sufficiently like his stolen ID to pass.

At the junction with the Amur, there was a modern concrete marina on the south side of the Bureya, which serviced the river freighters and barges, and a smaller wooden one on the north with the name of Karamazov's that was favored by locals. Stopping there, he pulled up to the dock with the gas pump, unloaded his empty cans, and waited for an attendant. Karamazov himself came down to greet his new arrival.

"I need fuel and supplies," Petrov informed the older man. He looked like he was of mixed White Russian descent with a tanned, weather-beaten face and shortish beard, dressed in rubber boots and a weather-proof jacket.

"How will you pay? I take hides, ivory, gold, rare woods, and rubies, if you have any," he informed as he looked over the tightly tarped bundles in the boat.

"I have rubles," Petrov replied. "I need enough fuel and food to last me about a week."

"Rubles, you say. Really," Karamazov replied with enthusiasm because he was typically fur-rich and ruble-poor. "I'll have my boy get your supplies while I fuel you up."

Karamazov pressed a button on a post, and shortly, a figure came down the dock who had a missing left arm and scarred face.

"Give him a list of what you want, and he will bring it down to you. We get all sorts here, and it does not pay to leave a boat unattended," Karamazov replied as he gave Petrov a pad and pencil to write on before he started filling the cans. "First, I need to see an ID."

Petrov pulled the red internal passport out of his pocket and handed it over. He had spent hours making up a backstory that he was Paul Glavinovitch, who had been run out of his home because of a disagreement with his stepfather and had spent the winter trapping, and he never intended to go home again.

"You don't look much like your picture?" Karamazov questioned.

"That's what I looked like without a beard and with a shaved head. That's me all right. That's why I left. My stepfather wanted to send me into the army," Petrov explained. "I took my dad's boat, traps, and left. I will never go back."

"There is a lot of that going around," Karamazov said. "I'll sell you your gas, and you were never here. Putin takes our sons, and most come back in wooden boxes. Heroes, he says. A few, like my son, will never be the same. All heroes fighting to liberate the Ukrainians from Fascism, and protect the Russians there from unspeakable horrors, or so they say. There are only Russians in Ukraine, so they tell us on the radio. Oh yes, and they keep telling us and sending us back boxes and damaged heroes. I have said too much."

Petrov desperately wanted to know what was happening in the war in Ukraine, but dared not ask Karamazov. What he longed for was fresh milk, real rye bread, chocolate candy with hazelnuts, canned corned beef, pickled herring, limes, flour, some fresh pastries like those from the bakery at home, and cigarette lighters so that he did not have to start fires with flint and steel. For news, maybe Karamazov's son could tell him something, or he could ask for recent newspapers or magazines.

After his son had brought down the groceries in a cart, Karamazov tallied up the totals on his abacus for 23 liters of gasoline and his supplies, which came to 8,250 rubles. With the mix of bills, he paid Karamazov, and Petrov and his son loaded the boat.

Petrov offered his helper one of the candy bars and said, "I have not spoken to anyone all winter. I'm desperate for news. Can you tell me what's going on in Ukraine? I'll pay 50 rubles. I need to know."

Petrov watched as Karamazov's son slowly and apparently painfully chewed on the candy bar and motioned for some of the milk to wash it down. When he had finished, he started to speak. "I believed what they told us and volunteered. We went through training at a base near Vladivostok and were told that we would be welcomed as liberators and the war would be over in two weeks. The Ukrainians had built layers of trenches and fought back with mines, drones, tanks, everything. Many of my friends were killed. We were ordered to destroy everything. We shelled homes, blew up churches, and were ordered to shoot anyone who opposed us in any way. We shot women and children. We took the youngest and sent them to be raised by families in Russia. We raped, stole, destroyed, pillaged, and burned. What we could not take, we ruined. Strange thing that. After all we did for them, the Ukrainians did not want to be Russians."

"I see," Petrov replied. "Were there any here that you know of that resisted being inducted?"

"There was one from upriver somewhere. He supposedly killed a commissar and two men. They had wanted posters up for him with a 50,000-ruble reward, dead or alive. I suppose that he is still out there somewhere. He sounds dangerous."

"Do you have a poster? I'd like to know what he looks like in case I run into him?" Petrov asked as casually as possible.

"No. My father burned them all. He said that they made a good fire starter."

"I see," Petrov answered. "Thank you. Push me off. I want to make as many miles as I can before I lose the light."

******

Petrov was on his way once more. The Whirlwind purred along on the fresh fuel, skirting the fuel tanker and river freighters that were tied up across the river. Only once before had he been on the Amur with his father. It was deep, fast, and wide enough that whitecaps could form on windy days, to say nothing of the bow waves generated by the larger ships. Many of the ships and barges were tankers carrying fuel to isolated villages to replenish their supply. There was always a general sigh of relief when the tankers arrived, even if they were accompanied by politicians. They often promised much, but gave back as little as possible - maybe some candy or butter and perhaps a little cheap vodka for the headmen of the village.

He felt his little craft, large as it had been on the stream where he started, was like a grain of rice floating in a bathtub. He would have to make a spray shield to put over the bow to keep water out of the boat. There was no protection from the Spring thunderstorms. The best he could do was to tie up under the lee of a bank and wait them out while bailing the boat. Once, when a storm started late in the day, he pulled up to a bank, tied up the boat, stripped naked, and showered in the downpour. When it passed, he started a fire and dried everything out before proceeding. His camp looked like he was holding a fur auction with every nearby bush supporting animal skins.

Although he had discarded the rifles, he had kept the Makarov pistol. He knew that it would be of little use against the huge brown bear or tigers that inhabited the Bureya Nature Reserve. He had seen a bear scavenging the carcass of a winter-killed moose and had heard the roar of a tiger that was probably trying to get a deer. That sound sent chills down his spine. "Good luck on your hunt," he shouted. "Just don't eat me."

As fast as the furs dried, he took them down and wrapped them in tight bundles around which he lashed his tarps. Mildew was his enemy now, and it could ruin the furs in which he had invested an entire winter's work. He also did not want to be a target of river pirates who could attack at any time. He took the precaution of always having the pistol with him, even in his sleeping bag.

His thoughts wandered to an American movie he had seen, "The Adventures of Grizzly Adams," and he thought these adventures were not unlike his own. He supposed that he had a romantic streak in him, but realized that the movie was a fantasy. His problems were not with the American Indians, but with a police state whose tentacles were reaching every aspect of everyone's lives.

******

On his fifth night, he pulled up to an inviting sandy landing with a forested background and easily gathered enough wood for a campfire. He stretched a piece of tent fabric between two trees and cut some rushes for a mattress. He opened some tins of sardines that he had bought and enjoyed the last of his rye bread and cheese. During the last bit of daylight, he worked on a bow stave made from a limb of Osage orange. The tree had long since dropped its grapefruit-sized fruit, but with some arrows made of river cane and tipped with bone, stone, or metal points, it could silently take game animals and some of the spawning carp in the weed beds around the river. When darkness came, he pulled himself inside his sleeping bag and quickly fell asleep.

Suddenly, his bag was being violently shaken, and he felt teeth penetrating his left arm. Awakening, he realized that a brown bear had grabbed the side of the sleeping bag and was dragging him out of the shelter. He found the Makarov in his bag and fired a shot. The bear released him and fled with her yearlings following behind. He smelled burning and realized that his sleeping bag was on fire. Disregarding the pain in his arm and blood spurting from a bleeding foot, he wiggled out of the bag and stood away as the burning bag ignited the oiled canvas of his shelter. As the rushes he had gathered started to catch fire, he reached under and grabbed his boots, burning his hand in the process. Only then did he notice the blood spurting from his foot.

Using his bow stave to support himself, he staggered back into the boat. He took his belt and tightened it around his ankle, and pushed out into a quiet eddy in front of the beach. As best he could with one functional arm and one functional leg, he poured vodka over his foot, bandaged it, and drank a good slug to deaden the pain.

"Help. Over here," he shouted when he saw a man in a canoe pulling his net after a night's fishing.

"After I get my fish in," the man replied as he pulled one side of the net, hooked it, and then pulled the other side – alternating back and forth. He was one small brown man doing the work of two. One of his fish was a huge Amur carp that was nearly a meter and a half long, which was about as long as the fisherman was tall. Nonetheless, he set his gaff and pulled it aboard. After he had a load of carp and suckers in the boat, he motored over to Petrov.

Supposing that this was a Nanai fisherman, Petrov spoke to him in that language. "I was attacked by a bear. I need help."

"Are you bleeding?" Mikhail Dulikan asked.

"Not so much now," Petrov relief. "I have a hurt arm and foot. I can't walk. There is a pistol where the fire was. Can you get it?"

"Tomorrow. Now we must get you to my wife. She can fix you up. Pull your motor out of the water. I will tow you back," Mikhail replied.

******

As he approached their camp, he could see a landing area where the bank had been dug away so boats could be pulled onto the shore. Behind it was a series of pulleys attached to a stout birch to allow canoes to be pulled out of the river onto the higher bank. He watched helplessly as Mikhail first beached his boat, pulled it up, and then returned to retrieve his craft. He was welcomed by Buran, the family's Laika, who barked excitedly to announce his master's return. The red and white furred dog had its tail curved over its back, and its powerful forequarters indicated that this was a working dog and a hunter. He eyed the following canoe with suspicion and bristled as he saw the large white man in the rear of the boat. Petrov was glad that he had the length of the boat between him and the dog until introductions could be made.

"Down, Buran. Down. It's all right. He's a friend," Mikhail commanded.

Buran did not appear to be convinced. Although he sank down on his stomach, his teeth were still bared, and he issued a low growl.

Mikhail stroked Buran's fur and gave him a slab of dried fish that he grabbed off the drying rack, which the dog chewed as his master started winching Petrov's canoe up the ramp.

By the time Petrov was abreast of the dog, Buran had finished his meal, but his ears were still laid back and his lips pulled up to reveal his white teeth. Petrov knew very well that Laikas would fight to the death to defend their families. He remained motionless until Mikhail came up and lifted Petrov's hand up for him to smell or chomp on, and Petrov did not know which, but he hoped for the former, rather than the latter. The dog rose to his feet, smelled the hand, and then jumped back.

"It's all right," Mikhail assured the doubting Petrov. "It just takes a little time for Buran to get used to new people."

By this time, Buran had been joined by Nina, Mikhail's wife, his eight-year-old son, Alexei, and his three-year-old daughter, Tanya, who came to help unload Mikhail's boat and prepare the morning's catch for drying.

"Nina, this man has been attacked by a bear. Help me get him inside. Alexei, start unloading the boat. I'll be back in a moment," his dad ordered.

Using a paddle as an improvised cane and supported by the couple, the three made their way up the ramp towards the "balagan," an octagonal wood and sod building that had not changed since the Stone Age. Except for the addition of a sheet metal stove and stove pipes that had replaced the central fire pit. Two glass windows, kerosene lamps, and metal cooking utensils were among the few other concessions to modernity. Wood, rocks, bone, sod, mud, moss, and hides were the structure's basic components.

"I must help my son with that big fish and get there before curiosity gets the better of him. Is there anything dangerous in your boat?" Mikhail asked.

"I have a couple of knives and an ax," Petrov responded. "There is some vodka in there, too. Please bring me some."

Nina shook her head. "We have better. Save that for later. Let's get you inside and look at your wounds."

After navigating the low doorway, Nina sat Petrov down on a wooden pole bed and started to help him get out of his shirt. When she lifted his arm, he cried out in pain. Taking a knife, she slowly undid Petrov's improvised bandages and cut off portions of his blood-soaked shirt. When she attempted to raise his arm, he nearly fainted. Underneath the bandage was a scabby mass of congealed blood, dirt, fabric, and leaves.

Turning her attention to his foot, she also had to cut the shoe away and the dried blood that had glued it to Petrov's foot, revealing a multicolored scab.

Tanya had been sitting nearby, observing everything.

"Tanya. Go get Buran and bring him inside," her mother ordered.

In answering a questioning look from Petrov, Nina said, "Buran will lick and clean your wounds while I gather some plants. Don't worry, Tanya will be here."

Tanya returned with Buran. She brought the dog in and pointed towards Petrov's foot. Petrov slowly extended his foot, saying, "Go ahead, Dr. Buran. You know what to do."

Looking at the underside first, Buran stood and started licking the side of the foot. The dog's tongue felt warm and generally relaxing. The pain in the foot decreased as it was being cleaned. As Buran worked, Petrov gently stroked the fur on his head and scratched him behind the ears. Buran's tail wagged in response. They were becoming friends.

Nina had cut fresh willow leaves and branches for antiseptic and boiled yarrow and birch to boil to make a warm compress to put on his foot and arm.

When Buran was finished, the dog went to the door and lay down with all its feet in the air and went to sleep. After Nina had put the compresses on his wounds, Petrov quickly fell asleep. For the first time since he left home, he felt warm and safe.

CHAPTER 4

UNDER PROTECTION

As comfortable as Petrov was during the three weeks he spent with Mikhail's family. He knew that his presence was a danger to them, and he must be on his way. With Nina's herbal treatments and Dr. Buran's attentions, his injuries were mending. For the first week, he could not even wipe his ass because he could not support himself on his good arm and single leg while taking a crap. Nina had done that function for him as well as washed his entire body in full view of the inquisitive children who were fascinated by his pale skin, larger body, and, to his considerable embarrassment, his genitalia.

Sleeping in a single room where everyone performed all aspects of their body functions during the deep winter months in view of everyone else took a bit of adjustment for Petrov. When he had morning erections, he had to relieve those as discreetly as possible. Mikhail and Nina had sex several times a week. When they did, Petrov turned away from them in their bed, less than a meter away. The children ignored their parents' sexual activities as this was to them an everyday activity, like cooking or chopping wood.

The last night before he left, he felt the covers pulled back, and Nina was standing naked beside his bed. As Mikhail watched, she proceeded to unbutton Petrov's shirt. Shocked, Petrov looked over to Mikhail, who spread his hands out, wiggled his fingers, and made a back-and-forth motion in an unmistakable gesture that they were to make love and that it was all right. He was extending the ultimate measure of hospitality, and it would be an insult for Petrov to refuse.

Submitting, he undid his belt and wiggled out of his trousers as Nina pulled them. Then, as he sat up, she finished removing his shirt and undershirt. With her small hands, she fingered his nipples and then leaned over to flick them with her tongue and kiss them. A rising bulge in his underwear was an ample signal of his increasing readiness. She removed his underpants, and the erection sprang up to her delight. She wrapped her hands around the throbbing shaft and bent over to see it rise again. She then got on top and put it inside her.

Petrov felt the warm glide of his penis entering Nina's body, and he arched his back to provide a stronger thrust as she pushed herself up and down. Soon, in synchronous movement, they proceeded until he ejaculated. Nina also climaxed and then collapsed on top of him. Petrov wrapped his arms around her and held her until she recovered and slid away to return to her husband.

As he turned his head, he saw that Alexei and Tanya had been watching along with Mikhail. What could he ever say to them? Everyone had seen everything.

The next morning, Mikhail greeted him with a beaming smile, a chuckle from Alexei, and a giggle from Tanya as Nina went about her morning activities, and he started to get ready to leave his newfound family.

For Petrov to make it any further down the Amur, he needed to replace his long-shafted engine with one having a vertical propeller for more efficient operation. Then he could sit while operating the boat, rather than having to stand all the time, which carried the additional risk of being thrown overboard by a sudden impact or wave.

"It is time to take your furs to market," Mikhail confirmed. "It is a little late, but there are still fur buyers in Khabarovsk. Some Chinese buyers will give you the best prices for your ivory. I also have some furs. We will go downriver with both boats, and from there you can go to Birodidzhan and continue your journey."

"I am going to need a new engine to give me better control and more power on the Amur. For all you have done, I would be happy to give you this one for you to have or trade for something else," Petrov offered.

"I'd like another Whirlwind. Then I'd have spare parts when I need them," Mikhail suggested.

"Done then. We'll both leave with new engines," Petrov agreed.

"There is someone I know who will buy your ivory. They call him 'The Merchant.' Lang Wei is his name. He has a contact point outside of town. We'll call him and arrange for a meeting. He pays in rubles," Mikhail informed him. "I'll call and see if we can trade with him. If we can't, we'll find someone else."

As they prepared to leave, Petrov noticed that Mikhail and Nina were working on a small figure. This was an ongon, which was a smaller representation of the bone and wooden house shrine on the east side of the house. With a humanoid head and dressed in split skins, and having tufts of hair and feathers. It represented Domovoi, the guardian spirit of the home and family, of which Petrov was now a member, and was to be awarded protection on his journey.

"Keep him with you always," Nina admonished. "Respect and honor him. He will keep you safe."

Petrov bowed in reverence and sincerely thanked Nina for this gift of their faith, which had its origins thousands of years before Christ. As he carefully placed the doll-like figure in a protected spot in the front of his Amurisky, he thought, "I need all the help that I can get."

After five days of travel on the Amur, Mikhail pointed to a rocky point overlooking the river where a wind-blasted spruce tenaciously hung onto a glacier-carved bedrock hill. "That is the place. I'll call and see if we can sell to Wei."

Climbing to the top of the granite knob, Mikhail found a flip phone concealed in the tree's trunk and pushed the single call button. He quickly got a response.

"What do you have?" a gruff-voiced voice asked in Russian.

"Furs and ivory," Mikhail replied.

"Proceed downriver five kilometers. Look for a ship with a green, red, and gold trading flag," the anonymous voice directed.

After Mikhail returned and they resumed their journey, Petrov felt something that he had never experienced before. This was a feeling of eager anticipation as if waiting for time to open a Christmas present, but it was even more than that. He had taken pride before when he under his father's tutelage had been paid real money for fixing something a villager owned. This was different. For the first time, he was to be paid for work that he did by himself. He had trapped the animals, prepared the hides, found the ivory, gotten them safely down two of Russia's major rivers, survived a bear attack, and was going to be paid like a man. A real man out on his own in the world. This was a rite of passage, and if it came off successfully, he would have passed this test of his own making. He had been severely challenged and had nearly succeeded.

******

When they rounded a bend, Petrov saw a river freighter tied up in quiet water behind a bluff. It was rusted with peeling paint that looked like an organic part of the landscape, except for a whisp of smoke coming from its stack. The trading flag was two meters long and hung from the stern, and the gangway had been lowered to accept visitors. As they approached, three men came down to welcome them.

An imposing man stood in the middle of the gangway and motioned to spots where the two canoes could be tied up. This was a routine activity for Demetri Grigoryev, who had been Wei's Number-One man for over a decade. After the boats were secure, he extended his arm down to Mikhail and helped him onto the dock. Petrov also accepted his help as his legs had become somewhat unsteady after hours of river travel.

"Come aboard. My men will take your goods up to the fur buyer, and Wei will see you in about an hour after your furs are graded. He will examine the ivory when you meet. You will need to give me any weapons before you come aboard," Demetri informed the pair.

Petrov handed over his belt knife and Makarov pistol, and Mikhail gave up his knife.

Examining the burned exterior of the pistol and its ivory grips, Demetri remarked, "This pistol has seen some action."

"Yes, it has. It was burned in a fire, but it shoots fine. Try it out if you like, but please replace any ammunition that you shoot," Petrov replied.

Although the exterior of the vessel was nondescript to the point of being shabby, the interior was richly appointed. Demetri ushered the pair into a dressing room where they could shower and change into robes.

"When you are done, relax here. There are cigars from Cuba and brandy if you like. I'll come for you when Wei is ready. I'll have your clothes taken care of and call for a barber if you want," Demetri offered.

"I would like a haircut and beard trim. My boots were damaged. I would also like a new pair of work boots, if that can be managed?" Petrov replied.

"Take your time with your shower. I'll send the barber in about 15 minutes. Give me your boot, and I will have the store clerk fit you out with a pair. We have brown and black. Which do you prefer?" Demetri informed.

"I'll have the black ones," Petrov replied.

Although Nina and Buran had done their best to clean Petrov up, the feel of warm, flowing water on his body and using real soap to clean himself felt so relaxing that he was in danger of falling asleep. The stream of water on the nape of his neck was so sleep-inducing that he turned the shower to cold to wake himself up. Satisfied that he smelled a little less like a walrus, he dried himself and put on the thick terrycloth robes and selected a pair of embroidered slippers with non-skid soles suitable for the polished wooden floors. He looked longingly at the brandy, but Mikhail stopped him.

"No brandy," Mikhail warned. "You will want to be sharp when we talk to Wei."

In a state that could only be called luxurious compared to their camps, the pair settled down in deep green leather chairs that were trimmed in gold braid. The auspicious colors of green, red, and gold were repeated in the decor as if this were an anteroom in a large hotel. Warm, clean, and relaxed, Petrov enjoyed the experience. Mikhail was more alert in these unfamiliar surroundings and commented. "After being treated like this and getting half drunk on the brandy and cigars, people will agree to almost anything. He is a sharp, but fair, trader. He has built a reputation for being honest, but ruthless to anyone who crosses him. You will impress him if you are forthcoming and honest about your answers. He is said to never forget a face."

When Demetri escorted them into the trading room, Petrov was struck by its opulence. It was paneled with dark rosewood and centered in the room was a highly polished rosewood table carved with koi, dragons, and phoenixes while the proceedings were being watched over by an antique bronze Buddha, a richly dressed Ganesha, and overseeing all Guan Yu with his stern face, armor, and Green Dragon Crescent Blade "guan dao" which bespoke honesty, straight dealing, and fidelity. An oriental rug with gold and silver threads depicting gardens of plenty covered much of the floor. The smell of sandalwood arose from the incense sticks burning at the Buddha. Spread across the top of the large table, his tusk sections were laid out along with the Makarov pistol with its ivory grips.

Wei appeared to be in his mid-50s. He was dressed in a sharply cut blue naval captain's jacket with gold buttons and gold braid on its shoulder boards and sleeves. He had the look of a Captain in command. Although not as tall as Petrov, he was solidly built with broad shoulders that tapered down to a thin waist. He rose and bowed slightly to the pair.

"Mikhail. It is good to see you again. I see that you have brought a friend, whom I suspect I know of, but have never met. Petrov, is it not?" Wei asserted.

"Yes, I am."

"It was reported that you are wanted in connection with the deaths of your father, a commissar, and two troopers whose bodies were found in a burned-out building. Is that true?" Wei questioned.

"They killed my father, and I killed them. I spent the winter trapping and found the ivory that I brought. I was hurt by a bear, and Mikhail and his family took me in and nursed me back to health." Petrov admitted.

Mikhail was taken aback when he heard this information, and the expression on his face was instantly transmitted to Wei.

"So, you did not know that this person was a triple murderer?" Wei asked.

Unable to speak at first, Mikhail shook his head and replied, "He only told us that he wanted to escape to Ukraine and help stop Putin."

"Is this true. Is that your objective?" Wei asked harshly.

"Yes," Petrov replied. "I want to help stop what he is doing."

"Mikhail, there is a reward for this man. It is much more than the value of these furs. If you want, we will turn him in and arrange for you to get this money. Or we can proceed and get you both on your way," Wei proposed.

"I did not know that he had killed people. He expressed only kindness to my wife and children. We have taken him under the protection of our house. I value his friendship more than money," Mikhail replied as he looked at Petrov to see an expression of profound relief come over his face.

"Then, Mr. Petrov, you will be under my protection as well. Relax, you were never here. We have some business to do with your ivory. Unfortunately, you had to cut up this magnificent tusk, but it is of excellent quality. For the nine pieces you brought, I can give…" as Wei spoke, Petrov raised his hand.

"Mr. Wei, there were ten pieces, not nine. The smallest piece, the tip, is missing. They were all wrapped in the same tarp," Petrov reported.

"Demetri. See about this," Wei ordered.

Demetri turned and left the room. A few minutes later, a scuffle was heard on the deck, followed by a series of blood-curdling screams lasting some 15 minutes and the splash of something heavy being thrown overboard.

"Sorry for the interruption, gentlemen," Wei continued in a nonchalant voice. "Good help is hard to find."

A few minutes later, Demetri returned with the missing section of tusk wrapped in a towel and carrying a silver tray containing two severed hands holding a human heart. Wei nodded, and the tray was placed before the statue of Guan Yu, who appeared to Petrov to smile in satisfaction that justice had been done.

"The crew witnessed the punishment?" Wei asked.

"I used the tusk first, then the hands, and finally the heart," Demetri replied. "I don't think we will have any more thefts."

"Thank you, Demetri. Examples must be made. You can leave us now and clean up," Wei replied as he waved him away.

"Sorry for the interruption." Wei continued. "With the worldwide near-prohibition of the traffic of elephant ivory, high-quality Siberian ivory has fluctuated in price, but is generally on an upward trend, as there is still strong demand in China, India, and the Middle East, but declining in the United States and Europe. I can see how well it works from the pistol grips that you made. I assume that you probably want to sell the gun too, as it could be traced back to the army and the murders."

"Yes. That is correct," as Petrov said these words, he could imagine this pistol being found at a checkpoint and his being asked how he got it.

"Generally, the ivory is in excellent condition, but there are some internal cracks, and the rim on the outside of the tusk might conceal other flaws. With that additional piece, I can offer you 900,000 rubles," Wei explained.

"I worked that ivory when I made the grips," Petrov countered. "It carves very well and didn't have any soft spots. Perhaps I could sell you some of it and the remainder in Khabarovsk?"

"Perhaps you could if you could find the right people before you were killed," Wei advised. "Young man, I suggest that you get a bank card and carry as little cash as possible. I'll pay an additional 1000 rubles for the pistol."

Fur buyer Lie Shou came into the room with the tally sheets listing the furs and their value, and gave them to Wei. He was a slightly built man wearing traditional black trousers and a green over shirt with a floral print overhanging the pants.

"Although you have fewer furs, yours were well prepared, and some rated top quality. Your wolf furs were particularly nice. For your two wolf pelts, three martin, two mink, otter, beaver, and lynx, I can offer you 15,000 rubles," Wei explained.

"Trapping near my home is getting tough, as this area has been trapped for years," Mikhail explained. "With my fishing, I don't have as much time for it. Still, my family would welcome a little something extra."

"Mr. Petrov, you had more than twice the number of pelts, but they are not as well finished as Mikhail's, with some showing burn marks. For yours, the offer is 24,500," Wei concluded with a note of finality in his voice.

Petrov hesitated in his reply, but did not dare to prolong the discussion as he sensed that his host was getting impatient. "Perhaps with your connections, you could advise us where to stay in Khabarovsk, where they don't ask too many questions? Then I would be very happy to accept your offer and continue my journey."

Wei pressed a button on the table and withdrew a flat box such as might hold fine cigars and passed it to Petrov. When he opened it, Petrov found it contained identical gold rings with the top inlayed with the green, red, and gold stripes of Wei's trading flag.

"Select one and put it on your little finger," Wei stated. "The ring signifies that you are under my protection. Anyone who also has such a ring is honor-bound to render the service that you require if it is within their power. Present this at the Golden Dragon Inn, and they will take care of you for a week until you are ready to leave. They also have safe storage for your boats. I offer this to you and Mikhail in recompense for having one of my former employees attempting to steal your ivory."

"I am most grateful and honored to accept your offer and kindness," Petrov answered with a bow.

"You should leave now. You will notice my flag hanging on a dock on the west side of the river. Follow the channel by the dock, and that will take you to the lower levels of the hotel. I wish you both uneventful journeys," Wei rose as he spoke, indicating a scuffed-up duffle bag with a plastic bag inside that Shou was filling will stacks of ruble notes as they spoke.

"You may recount them if you wish," Shou advised. "I have put them in 1000-ruble bundles. The largest bills are 100-ruble notes that you can spend without attracting attention. I assure you that the count is correct. I suggest that you leave as quickly as possible. The waterway can be very dangerous after dark. For 10,000 rubles, I'll have one of our power boats tow you to the hotel. It will take two trips."

"Please arrange that," Petrov responded. "We did not come this far to risk everything at the end."

Demetri, now cleaned and redressed, rejoined the pair in the dressing room.

"Are there pirates on this part of the river?" Petrov questioned.

"Yes, there are, and we deal with them severely if we catch them, Demetri began. "The lucky ones are only shot to death, as for the others, we punish according to their complicity. For some, we only take an arm. For others, something more and over a longer period of time. As the boss said, it is important to make examples."

Petrov was to go first. As they stood on the dock, Mikhail spotted a film of blood on the surface of the water where minnows were feeding. "No one wants to cross Wei," Mikhail stated.

Petrov enjoyed his ride inside the power boat while his Amurisky bobbed happily behind. When he got to the dock, he was met by two men who tied up his boat as he waited for Mikhail. For the moment, they would continue their adventures together.

CHAPTER 5
THE YARMULKE TRADE

Approaching the river port at Khabarovsk, Petrov saw there were tugs, barges, and river freighters tied up to wharves on the west side of the river. He thought his Amurisky being towed behind the power boat must have felt as intimidated as he was by the larger vessels. He was a bit more confident in the power boat with its armed crew as they approached a slipway adorned with Wei's flag. Pulling in, Petrov returned to his canoe, where he was directed to a cavernous opening leading into a hill with the ten-story Green Dragon Inn spreading out on top. Compared to the church spires and brightly colored buildings dating from before the Revolution in the background, this was obviously a Stalinist structure. It was gray, drab, and boxy, with only the more numerous windows indicating that this building was designed to be a hotel, rather than a warehouse.

"I'll wait for my friend," Petrov told the dock man, who was in his 40s. He was wearing only shorts and a red soccer shirt emblazoned with bright yellow letters spelling out a local team's name.

"We'll go in together. He's a Nanai and not used to all this," Petrov explained.

"Very well, it will take about an hour for the launch to make a round trip. It's a pleasant day. You want a smoke?" the attendant offered.

"I have been out trapping all winter. What's been happening?" Petrov asked.

"SKA-Energiya-Khabarovsk won against Neftekhimik by only a single goal, but this makes five wins in a row. I think that they may be able to go places this year. Maybe even making the national playoffs," the attendant enthusiastically replied.

"I'm glad for you. You are obviously a fan. What's happening internationally?" Petrov probed.

"Our teams were banned from the Olympics, but somehow competed individually. They brought home some medals, and we are proud of them," he replied.

"What of Ukraine? Is the war still going on?" Petrov inquired.

"Yes, except it is not a war, and we are supposed to be winning. We are only there to help the Ukrainians throw off their Fascist dictator and get back what was once ours. It's said that we are receiving supplies and men from China and North Korea to help the fight. Every time I turn on the news, it is supposed to be over soon, but it keeps dragging on and on. I just don't know. Those who come back don't talk about it," he responded.

Once Mikhail arrived, they were directed to a cavernous underground structure where their canoes were cradled, lifted, and placed in cages nearly two floors above the water level.

"Take what you want out of the boats, close the door, and lock it by placing your hand on the screen," a voice from a speaker directed. "Put your bags into one of the carts, take the lift at the end of the passage to the lobby."

Their canoes were the smallest vessels in storage. There were several speedboats and two small cabin cruisers in other compartments. When the elevator door closed, the entire area was plunged into darkness.

"As soon as I get my engine, I'm leaving." Mikhail insisted. "Anyone could get killed here, and no one would ever know."

At the desk, the clerk greeted the travelers with a few words. "You are expected. Room 415. You may take your cart up and unload."

They were soon in their room, which was plainly furnished with light-colored wood panels arranged in a chevron pattern and blond furniture made of laminated bamboo. There were two beds, and a screen adorned with a painting of two cranes flying over forested peaks was folded against one wall. Prominently inset in one wall was a refrigerator-sized safe with the same type of hand-print lock as the boat cages.

Petrov heaved the 20-kilo bag onto the bed and spread the packages of used ruble notes on the bed. "Mikhail, I have never seen so much money in all my life – nearly a million rubles. Wei is right, I can't carry this with me, and I can't put it in a bank without identification. I've got it. I need it, but I don't know what to do with it. It will have to go into the safe for now."

"You could put it into diamonds, like the Czar had sewn into his family's clothes, but no one would give you what they were worth if you needed money in a hurry," Mikhail offered. "You can't use that ID you took because that would lead the police straight to you. I'm confident that another idea will suggest itself."

"I hope so. I can't travel with this much cash." Petrov mused. "I can't hide it forever, and I can't buy anything with such a large amount of money without drawing suspicion."

The following morning, they took the boats to a marina that sold Whirlwind products. One motor in a packing box was stored in Mikhail's canoe, while a straight-shafted version was attached to Petrov's.

Mikhail's departure was brief as he wanted to make it as far upriver as daylight would allow.

"I certainly want to thank you for all you and your family have done for me," Petrov began. "If it wasn't for you, Nina, the children, and Buran, I wouldn't have made it this far."

"Enough, or I will cry. Nina feels like you have given us a big, strong son to look after us in our old age." Mikhail replied. "You have freely given of yourself. Nothing more can be asked. You are family now. I am sorry that you must leave us, but I know you must go. May the Gods protect you. Goodbye." With an awkward embrace, Mikhail hugged Petrov, got into his canoe, and departed up the dark river towards home.

Petrov felt a sinking feeling in his stomach as he watched his friend, who had been an unexpected mentor and sage, depart up the dark river. He was glad that he snuck a bundle of ruble notes into Mikhail's clothing as he packed. He also thought about the possibility that he might have a son that he would never know if Nina was right. Maybe she had the gift of foresight or perhaps more insight into the natural world. If there was to be a son, and he found himself hoping there would be, he felt that he would be raised in good hands.

Although within a city surrounded by tens of thousands of people, Petrov felt very alone when he went into the Green Dragon's bar. There was only a single customer who, judging from the number of glasses on the table, had been drinking for some time. His black Borsalino was halfcocked back on his head while the fringes of his tzitzit hung beneath his now wrinkled black coat and white dress shirt.

Hearing someone pull back a bar stool, the man spoke, "Have a drin… drink. Yeah, a drink. I'm going into the Army to die for the Mother… Father… land or something like that. Drink and be merry, for tomorrow I … I forget."

"I will be happy to drink with you," Petrov responded. "Being called to serve Mother Russia is a great honor. You will be a hero."

The figure on the stool braced himself with both hands on the edge of the bar and turned to look at Petrov.

Petrov was shocked. Although the dress and hair were different in style, it was like he was looking into a mirror. Petrov's complexion was darker, and his eyes were green rather than brown, but their facial features were identical. He had heard of doppelgangers but never imagined that he had one. As far as he could tell from this slumped-over figure, they were the same height.

The bartender brought Petrov a vodka, but said to the other patron, "Pay up and get out before you puke all over my bar. If you want to drink yourself to death, do it somewhere else."

Letting go of the bar with one hand, he attempted to retrieve his billfold from an interior coat pocket and started slipping off the stool. Petrov caught him and pushed him back to the bar.

"Thank you, Brother," he said as the teetering figure moved his head back and forth in an attempt to get a better look at his benefactor's face.

"I see you are his brother," the bartender said. "Pay up and get him out of here."

Pulling bills from the drunk's billfold while still supporting his newfound brother, Petrov said, "Take what you need, and enough to forget that we were ever here."

"No one is ever here. The elevator in the corner will take you to your room," the bartender informed and pocketed his tip.

Petrov walked and half-drug the figure to the elevator while the bartender brought the drunk's coat and hat. When he unlocked the elevator, he handed Petrov a half-liter bottle of Rasputin Vodka, which Petrov acknowledged with thanks. However, if things worked out, he would probably need it. He remembered his dad making what he called a Red Winter Cure, made by mixing vodka and pomegranate juice to which he added a pickle spear and a sprinkle of salt. In fact, he liked the remedy so much that he would sometimes drink it even if he didn't have a hangover.

As he entered the room, he felt his guest's body start to convulse. He rushed him to the commode, where he pulled down his pants, sat him on the seat, and put a trash can between his legs. He almost threw up from the repulsive acid odors erupting from the man who had now become his patient. He gave him a bottle of water to rinse his mouth, which provoked another round of discharges as the body tried to rid itself of accumulated toxins. After opening the window, he stripped off his guest's remaining clothes, pulled back the covers, and put him into the bed. Finally, he cleaned up everything and started going through the man's papers.

This was Yoni Rabbivinovitz. He was the same age as himself and in three days was to report to the Induction Center in Khabarovsk for processing. Although the irony of the possibility was not lost on Petrov, he could take this man's place and, if sent to Ukraine, find an opportunity to defect.

He rang the desk and asked that bread, cheese, pomegranate juice, pickle spears, salt, and boiled chicken breast be sent to the room. He also said that he had dirty laundry that needed to be processed that evening. In an hour, the bellman arrived, and Petrov could go to bed.

Petrov was awakened by a groan from the next bed and found Yoni gently feeling his head with both hands as he feared that it might explode. Petrov took a pillow from his bed and approached him. He could smother this man, have the body dumped into the river, and no one would ever know.

As he approached, he could see fear on Yoni's face as he responded, "No. We'll pay you," remembering a snatch of what happened the night before.

Petrov gently lifted Yoni's shoulders and put the pillow behind them so that he could sit erect in the bed.

"I've got to get to the bathroom," Yoni slurred as he pulled the covers back and found that he was naked.

"Who? What?" he asked, his speech stumbling to make his inquiry as his brain rushed through possibilities – all of which were bad.

"We'll talk later," Petrov assured. "Let me help you. I don't think you are ready to go anywhere right now."

Yoni tried to get up, but collapsed back onto the bed. Putting an arm around his back, Petrov walked Yoni to the commode and sat him down. "When you finish, I'll give you something to help,"

Making his best guess at his dad's hangover cure, he mixed two drinks and gave Yoni one, and tore off a piece of bread. "There is also some chicken and cheese when you feel like you can keep them down. I'll leave you alone now. Call me when you want to come out."

Petrov dressed and had his breakfast while Yoni finished in the bathroom. When Yoni emerged, he was wearing a towel and clung unsteadily to the door. Strategically, he stumbled from one piece of furniture to another until he found the bed and sat down.

"Thanks. That helped. Can I have another?" Yoni asked.

"No. Just some water and bread now. We need to make sure that what you ate will stay down," Petrov advised.

"Where's my phone. I need to call my dad and let him know that I'm all right," Yoni asked.

"I've got it," Petrov replied. "I can help you out of your situation, but we have to talk. I have some problems too, and I think that maybe we can work together. What is your problem?"

Yoni rubbed his head before he began. "I have been in training to be a Rabbi all my life. I was to go to New York to continue my studies, and my visa was approved. Then this notice to report to the Army was received. I don't want to kill Ukrainians, and I don't want to kill Palestinians either. I want to go to America and attend rabbinical school. I went to the bar in hopes of finding a smuggler."

"I know someone who can get you out through China. What I need is a new identity. I will go into the army in your place. Can your father help with that?"

"My family has been merchants in this town for generations. If we can convince my dad that your scheme will work, he knows people who can provide you with official IDs and whatever else you need."

After dwelling on the matter for a few minutes, Petrov gave Yani his phone and told him, "Assume that your phone is bugged. Just tell your dad that you are all right, and you will be bringing someone home for him to meet. We should be there by lunch."

Petrov went to the hotel barber and got a beard trim and his head shaved. He then went to the adjacent clothing store where he was fitted with a business suit, overcoat, and hat. He now looked like a young business executive and less like a half-drowned river rat that had crawled out of the town's sewers. Mentally, he complimented Wei on having everything in the hotel that might be needed to make whatever personal transformations a guest might need.

In the lobby's general shop, he also found colored non-prescription contacts and purchased three sets of brown lenses along with fluid. "Wei had indeed thought of everything," he marveled.

******

Located on a rise in the Jewish quarter of the city, Moishe Rabbivinovitz's house was a multistory mansion with a stucco exterior accented by brick outlined tall windows on the first floor and round windows on the second. The porch was supported by round stone columns atop a flight of seven steps from which one could view under-story windows, which partly illuminated the basement. A brick-lined moat-like structure filled with small, round river rock surrounded the house to provide drainage for the winter's rain and snow melt, which was shed by a steep, dark metal shingled roof.

"I've never seen anything like that," Petrov remarked.

"My grandfather had it put in," Yoni explained. "That drain is decorative, uses local materials, and at the time was less expensive than installing a tile drainage system, which had to come all the way from Moscow. It works and puts the water into a cistern."

As the doorman let them in, Petrov noted the thick walls that allowed two sets of windows. The exterior windows were heavier, and the interior set opened into the room.

Noting his interest, Yoni volunteered, "The windows are very practical. The outside ones shed snow, the space between them is filled with straw during the winter to stop the cold, and with screens in the summer to keep the mosquitoes out."

"Yoni, Yoni," Petrov chuckled. "This was not like the cabin where I spent the Winter or the one-room 'balagan' where I stayed when I was injured. That was like a yurt, but built of wood, moss, stone, bone, and hides. I survived both, but I don't know about this."

Petrov's feelings of displacement were reinforced by the grand entrance hall, which was terminated by a marble staircase leading to the upper story.

The doorman led the pair through the lower part of the house to a room facing an interior garden. On knocking at the door, a gruff "Enter" was heard, and the pair was ushered inside.

Moshi Rabbivinovitz was formally dressed in a suit and tie. Although his head was uncovered, the 65-year-old wore his skullcap pinned to his greying hair.

"Yoni, it is about time I heard from you," he scolded. "I was up most of the night worrying about you. I assume that you had success at the Green Dragon Inn?"

"More than I hoped for," Yoni began. "This man, who looks much like me, is willing to take my place in the Army. For his own reasons, he wants to get to Ukraine, and impersonating me is the safest way for him to travel. He needs new identification papers."

"Young man, are you a fugitive of some sort that you need a new identity?" Moshi questioned.

"Yes. The authorities are after me. I can put you in touch with a smuggler named Lang Wei who can get your son out of the country. I need a new internal passport and enough information that I can pass as your son," Petrov stated as dispassionately as he could, although he could detect a note of pleading in his voice.

"How can this work?" Moshi started. "We will have to come up with a story to explain how Yoni got more muscular and tanned and do something about your eyes. His eyes are brown. Yours are green."

"I have some contacts to take care of that. If we are talking negatives," Petrov added, "I'll also have to pick up enough Yiddish to at least know some common phrases and an explanation as to why I don't speak it."

"And how much is this going to cost me?" Moshi queried.

"I have no idea what Wei might charge. I have money, but I need to set up a bank account at Sberbank, and I need new identity documents for that."

"And just how did you come by this money? Did you steal it?" Moshi questioned.

"I was out trapping all winter," Petrov offered while attempting to be as truthful as possible. "I sold my fur and also a big mammoth tusk that I found to Wei. That's how I know him. Most of this money was honestly earned. A smaller portion I took from some men who attempted to kill me…"

"Stop. Enough. I believe you," Moshi ordered.

******

The gray concrete of the building housing the Ministry of Internal Affairs on Muravyov-Amursky Street contrasted strongly with the fairytale appearance of the old part of the city. Escaping from the ravages of World War II and now modified by murals created by the local artistic community, it was as if Czarist Russia had survived, although concessions to its wartime transformation into an industrial city were obvious.

They walked down the long corridors to the office of Col. Viktor Andreyevich, who headed the Migration Department, entered his office, and Moshi gave his card to the receptionist. Petrov hoped that the butterflies that he was feeling in his stomach were not too obvious.

"Colonel Andreyevich is on a call at the moment," the young receptionist replied, "I'll tell him you're here as soon as he is done."

A few minutes later, Andreyevich came out and greeted his old friend, "Moshi, it's good to see you. What do you need?"

"Victor, this is my son Yoni," Moshi began. "He has received orders to report for his army service. He was so eager to go that he had his head shaved, and now he looks nothing like his passport. He has been in a timber camp all winter to get physically fit and is tanned and more muscular than before."

"I agree. I would not have recognized him. Yoni, how are you? I have watched you grow up, but would not know you now," Andreyevich inquired.

"It was an exciting winter. Growing up in the city, I did not realize what it was really like out there. I was attacked by a bear, but my comrades saved me," Petrov replied in his new identity as Yoni.

"Very well, we will get started. It usually takes a month to get everything processed. I can perhaps do it now, but it will cost a little extra," Andreyevich responded.

"Moshi withdrew an envelope from his pocket and passed it across the table. "I trust this will cover everything."

Andreyevich opened the envelope, thumbed through the banknotes, and slid the packet into his drawer.

"Let's step down the hall for your photo and fingerprints, and then we may proceed. I assume that the address and kindred information on your old passport is correct?" Andreyevich asked.

"Yes," Moshi affirmed, "He's gained a little weight and perhaps some height, but everything else should be the same."

Returning, Andreyevich sat at his computer and recorded the new biometric information. "You said that you had been attacked by a bear. Do you have any scars?"

"On my right biceps and another on my foot from the bear's teeth," Yoni answered.

"I have an error message on your application. The fingerprints do not match. Can you explain?" Puzzled, Andreyevich posed this question, which had never occurred before.

Exhibiting his burned hand, Yoni replied, "I burned my hand attempting to put out a fire. I guess that is the reason that the prints might not look the same," Yoni responded.

Superimposing both sets of prints on his screen, Andreyevich turned to Yoni and replied. "Just so. Except for the scars, they are very close indeed. I'll put a note in the system. Your new passport will have the new prints. You should have your new passport in a few minutes."

Moshi and Yoni stood dumfounded but had to restrain their questions while they waited. With the match of fingerprints and their nearly identical appearances, Petrov and Yoni were undoubtedly brothers. Bursting with questions, they tried to act like they were going through an ordinary bureaucratic event, rather than having received earthshattering news.

A half-hour later, the assistant walked in with the new dark burgundy passport with its gold two-headed eagle and gave it to her boss.

"Moshi, I wish every father had prepared his son so well to defend our country. I am sure that he will have a long and glorious career. Yoni, the best of luck to you and stay safe," Andreyevich concluded as he rose.

"Colonel Andreyevich, could I have the old one?" Moshi asked. "Yoni is my only son, and I want to keep this memento of his life as he grew into a man."

"We are supposed to shred these," Andreyevich replied. "We honor our heroes after they are dead. I'll let you honor yours while he yet lives. Here, take it."

Moshi took the passport and placed it in his pocket. "Thank you for humoring an old man who is missing his son already."

Once back in the car, questions started to pour out of Petrov. "Who? What? How? He blurted out."

With a look of earnest regret, Moshi began, "When Yoni was born, we were told that there were twins and that one had died. We never saw the body. At that time, it was very difficult for hospitals out here, and white, healthy babies were valuable. Since we had one healthy child, the hospital sold you to the people you knew as your parents to help keep the hospital open. No one was ever told, and the entire business was kept secret. We can't tell anyone either. Not even your mother and Yoni. It is too dangerous for them to know."

"Somehow I think we knew," Petrov-Yoni responded. "Even when he was blind drunk, he called me brother. I had feelings for him that I have never felt for a man when I cared for him. That's what it was, brotherly love."

"I am sure that all that is true, but we must never speak of it again, and you are not to see him again lest he suspect that you really are his brother. This is for everyone's safety," Moshi affirmed.

******

Leaving the Municipal Building, the pair drove to the nearest Sberbank branch, which was in a sleek glass and steel building with a large green LED panel featuring a green circle and white check mark.

"We don't have my money," Yoni said.

"I don't want to explain how you came by that much cash. How much do you have left." Moshi asked.

"About 750,000 rubles, I suspect. I spent some on my new boat motor and clothes," Yoni replied.

"Very well. It will be easier for me to start your card with a transfer of funds from one of my accounts. That sounds more reasonable under the circumstances," Moshi concluded.

Once inside, they went to a kiosk and entered "new account" and received a number. Shortly, a man dressed in a tweed jacket came to them.

"Hello. Welcome to Sberbank. You wish to open an account?" the bank official asked.

"Yes, my son is going into the Army, and I would like for him to have a prepaid bank card that he can draw on when he needs money. He leaves the day after tomorrow, so we don't have much time," Moshi explained.

"Certainly. No Problem. Just step in here with me. This should take only a few minutes," the official assured as he motioned them into a small office space.

Once settled in and Moshi and Yoni had given the official their passports, he went to work on his computer, identifying Moshi's account and asking, "How much do you want to transfer?"

"One million rubles," Moshi replied.

Yoni moved to protest, but Moshi brought a finger to his lips to hush his response.

"Write down the password you wish to use and hand me the paper," the official requested.

Yoni did as he was bidden and shortly thereafter walked out with a card having a textured cover with the Sberbank logo and with his name, Yoni Rabbivinovitz, emblazoned on it. With each action, his transformation from Petrov to Yoni was becoming more complete.

******

In a hushed conversation in a room off the lobby of the Green Dragon Inn, Moshi, Yoni, and Petrov made the arrangements that Yoni would leave that night in Petrov's Amurisky with one of Wei's men. The Amurisky, with its new engine, would join Wei's fleet of vessels working the river.

As they parted, Petrov embraced Yoni and said, "I wish you every success and good luck, Yoni. We are both going to start new lives."

"And Brother, I also to you," Yoni replied. "Although we just met, I feel like you are a brother to me. I am going to try to be worthy of the danger that I am exposing you to."

"I had one son and now I have two, and I feel I am in danger of losing you both," Moshi said. "So now with my and God's blessings on you, go and do what you know is right."

CHAPTER 6

INDUCTION

Petrov was not cheered by his first view of the Eastern District Induction Center 46 in Birodidzhan. From the train, he saw a four-story gray concrete building with a parade field in front, surrounded by tall fences topped with coils of razor wire. At the station outside the camp, they were ordered into trucks and driven inside. Petrov felt a sinking feeling chew at his stomach as the driver closed the second of two camp gates with his remote control. He would have to be Yoni Rabbivinovitz every second of the day. He had almost broken his cover with a young woman on his two-hour train trip from Khabarovsk. He must not risk that again. Moshi had done his best to make a three-day Jew out of him. His newfound father said he would pack a trunk with books and clothes so he could play the part of a Rabbi's son. He would send it to him when he reached his duty post in Ukraine. For now, he could only carry a single bag.

In the false bottom of this trunk, he had carefully packed his radio components, not knowing if he would ever assemble them. That radio might be his path to escape or to his death if it were discovered.

In the second-class car, he took a window seat, and beside him was a talkative young woman who was peering wide-eyed out the window. She was wearing an often-mended coat belted around her slim waist, a blue flowered dress, and a hand-knit red scarf.

"It's wonderful out there. Look at all those houses, fancy buildings, and factories," Rina Goldstein gushed as she looked out the window and pushed on Yoni's shoulder.

"It's nothing special," Yoni replied. "Wait until we get to Birodidzhan. It's bigger with many more people."

"I'm sorry. I'm so excited. I have never been out of our village. This is all new to me. I'm Rina Goldstein," she explained.

"I'm Yoni. I lived in Khabarovsk and just spent a winter in the far north as a woodcutter. I haven't been to Birodidzhan either. It's a regional capital, so there are more people and things like operas, dance halls, movie houses, and bars."

"I knew it was the capital of the Jewish Autonomous Region. I learned that in school. Thank you very much. I hope that it has all you say and more. I want to see, feel, and smell them all. I want to know something besides cows, horses, and cabbage," Rina replied as she coughed from the smoke drifting over from the coal stove in the middle of the car.

"We are going for induction. I doubt that they will let us go to town. Maybe briefly before we leave?" Yoni suggested.

Another whiff of smoke came from the stove evoked a cough from Yoni, and when he lifted his hand to block his mouth, Rina saw that it was burned.

"You were in a fire?" Rina asked.

"Yes. It was at the logging camp. A lantern tipped over and set fire to the sleeping tent. The others and I got out. The tent was waxed, and it burned like a candle wick," Yoni explained as he made a mental note to remember this version of his story.

"I had some nurse training at the village clinic," she replied sympathetically. "I could have taken care of you."

"I'm sure you could," Yoni replied. "I'm tired and need some sleep. I'm sorry, but please let me rest. We are going to have a very busy next few days."

Rina nodded in assent. But her gaze was fixed on the window as forests of huge trees passed into moss-covered rocky tundra with snow-capped mountains in the background.

Arriving at the camp station at mid-morning, the inductees were lined up on the siding, ordered into trucks, and driven through the double pair of gates at the camp. Looking at the tangles of wire between the fences and at the tall guard towers, Yoni wondered, "This is more like a prison than a camp."

Isaak, who was sitting behind him, apparently had similar thoughts, but he expressed his out loud, "All this to keep us in?"

Looking back, Yoni saw an individual who was smaller than he was, pale-skinned, and had the long, delicate fingers of a pianist.

Making his best attempt to be an enthusiastic recruit, Yoni replied, "As loyal Russians, we must do what we can to protect our people against the Ukrainian Fascists who are suppressing Russians in Crimea."

"So, they tell us," Isaak replied with a notable lack of enthusiasm.

"Out. Out. Everybody Out. Take your bag and get out," Second-Rank Starshina Anstice barked as he walked into the back of the train car.

"That way, go out that way," He ordered as some tried to leave by walking past him. He ensured that nothing and no one was left behind.

Once outside the car, Petrov saw a line of trucks in front of the three train cars that were discharging their passengers. The trucks were high off the ground. Their tailgates were down, exposing rows of wooden benches. Two on each side and two down the central axis.

"Get in. Sit facing the front. Hurry. Hurry. People are waiting for you," the Starshina ordered.

Sitting pressed against the back of the person in front of him with another person behind him and with their bags piled between the rows of seats, he was glad that this would be a short trip. The weather was mild, so there was no tarp on the truck. With everyone clinging to their bags, they went inside the camp. He now knew how those Lithuanian herring felt when they were packed in their jars.

At the parade ground, they were met by a rank of bemedaled Starshinas in their dress uniforms, led by Fourth Rank Senior Starshina Boris Kaplan, who used a bullhorn to overcome the chatter of the group. "Line up in order of height. Tallest to my left and shortest to my right. Each Starshina will select his platoon and take them to barracks."

Petrov was the tallest member in his carload of inductees and was the first one approached by Starshina Kaplan. "What was your occupation?" he asked.

"I am a machinist and blacksmith. I spent last winter as a woodcutter in a logging camp," Petrov replied.

"Why is your head shaved?" Kaplan demanded.

"I wanted to be ready to do my duty," Petrov answered.

"Take off your shirt," Kaplan ordered.

Petrov complied and stood self-consciously as Kaplin looked him over like a side of beef.

Apparently satisfied with Petrov's muscular build, Kaplin ordered Petrov to put his shirt back on and step forward as he continued down the line.

Petrov noted that the Starshina selected a variety of individuals – not only the largest men. Two people he met on the train, Isaak and Rina, were among them. He found himself glad that Rina would be in his unit and mused that she might doctor on him yet.

Once inside the room in the large brick building that was to be their barracks while they underwent induction, they were allowed to unpack and stow their belongings in footlockers and hang a few things on a rack beside their bunks.

Kaplin came in and announced, "You will be here for two days. You will have your physicals in the morning, and if you pass, you will be issued uniforms and sworn in. Then you will go to a camp near Vladivostok for training. I will take you to the Mess Hall for supper. You will eat as a group and return as a group. Anyone who attempts to leave will be suspected of being a deserter and may be shot."

"You think that he means that?" Isaak asked as they sat down to eat a full meal of beef and cabbage with rye bread and pickles.

"I think that he does. They are not wearing those pistols as decorations," Petrov offered.

"At least they are going to feed us before they shoot us," Isaak replied.

It was still dark outside when Kaplan came to rouse his platoon. "Up. Up. You lazy bastards. To the Mess Hall for breakfast and then your physicals."

Petrov groggily remembered where he had put his clothes and pulled them on before they were formed into ranks and marched over the frosty ground to the Mess Hall, where an assortment of breads, cheeses, and hot barley cereal waited along with welcomed cups of tea.

Petrov sat beside Nikolai Sokolov, who was a White Russian with brown hair and a neatly trimmed beard. He was wearing fashionable jeans and an imported shirt. "If you play it right, you are going to be one of our corporals," he remarked.

"How do you know?" Petrov questioned.

"It's obvious. You are bigger, you have a commanding presence, and even though no one knows anybody yet, everybody regards you with a degree of respect," he informed the doubting Petrov.

"I don't know about that," Petrov rebuffed. "My father never thought that I would ever be anything but his assistant doing the grunt work of running a blacksmith's shop and fixing whatever the villagers brought to be repaired."

"I'll bet you a pack of American cigarettes that you make corporal before we are deployed," Sokolov said as he brandished a pack of Lucky Strikes still in their cellophane wrappings.

"I've never seen a pack. They must be worth 50 rubles?" Petrov guessed.

"Even more in camp. They are too valuable to smoke. Anyway, I like the Turkish ones better. They are even stronger than ours," Sokolov replied.

"How did you get those?" Petrov questioned.

"My father is Chief Gunsmith at the arsenal in Tula. He can get anything and send it to me. If there is anything you want, outside of women, I can have it in Siberia in two weeks," Sokolov explained.

******

Returning to barracks, they were ordered to remove their clothes and were escorted downstairs for their physicals. Going down the stairwell, another of his platoon, Yakov Zaytsev said, "Well, I hope everyone enjoys their 'Finger fucks', that's as close to having a woman that anyone is going to get around here."

Petrov soon learned what this was all about when he was sent into a room where a large Mongol woman put gloves on her hand, told him to bend over a table, and spread his buttocks as she probed his anus and fingered his prostate.

Seeing Yakov again in another line where they were drawing their clothes, Yani told him, "Now I know what you were talking about. I think they used the biggest woman they could find to do the exam."

"It's part of the bonding experiences that they are putting us through. Through shared trauma, intimidation, and pain, they are going to make a fighting unit out of us, whether we want it or not," Yakov explained. "I'm a psychiatrist, or at least I was, before they pulled me out of University."

With arms and butts sore from the shots, they returned to their barracks room to find that some of the bunks had been cleared by those who had failed their physicals. At least now they had their first issue of uniforms. These were striped colors of brown and green designed to blend with forest and tundra backgrounds.

"Put on your uniforms," Kaplin ordered. "You will go to the barbers, and then to lunch. In the morning, you will be sworn in and become members of the Russian Army, and we will depart for Vatisvostock."

******

The Starshinas arranged their troops in compact squares on the Parade Ground. Usually, a point and shout was sufficient to put them into a semblance of a military unit, but a few were grabbed by the shoulders and pushed into place.

"Silence!" Kaplin ordered. "You will be addressed by Comrade Colonel Vsevolod Mikhailovich Yegorov, who had retired to his dacha in Crimea when the Ukrainian Fascists took it, made a flowerpot of his beloved wife's funeral urn, and grew hemp which they watered with their urine. Should the Colonel ask you a question or make a comment, your answers will be, 'Yes, no, or I don't know, Comrade Colonel.' His only interest is that you are ready to kill any enemies of the state and die, if necessary, to do so."

A huge Russian Federation flag was hoisted on a flagpole. The historic tricolor of white, blue, and red was designed by Tsar Peter the Great and readopted by President Boris Yeltsin in 1993 after the former republics of the Soviet Union formed their own states. As the band played the national anthem, the words fixed like a burning brand in his brain. "Our free Fatherland, union of fraternal peoples, spaces for dreams, are open to all. Thus it was, thus it is, and thus it always will be. Loyalty to the Fatherland gives us strength. Using the wisdom of our forebears, be glorious. God be with you."

When each of the 13 guns on the field fired to welcome Colonel Yegorov, they drove the message of free, fraternal peoples being loyal to Russia's aims of peoples cooperating to have a glorious future, sanctioned by God, and not held by right of conquest, suppression, fear, and brutality as Putin was doing. His stepfather believed this too, and that was the "ancient wisdom passed onto him."

The Colonel arrived in a black Volga GAZ-21. His driver stopped beside the speaking platform, opened the rear door, and assisted Yegorov out of the vehicle onto the speaker's platform. Although Yegorov was a large man, the right side of his dark green tunic with its gold braid and buttons chest was only just large enough to hold the rows of metals hanging from his uniform. His work in the KBG had obviously been richly rewarded. He used his baton with its gold double-headed eagle of authority to accent his points as he spoke.

"Young men and women of the Russian Federation, you are being tasked with defending the Fatherland against the greatest threats since the end of the Great Patriotic War," he began. "Russians have been attacked in Crimea and have asked for our assistance to repel Ukrainians, who are now aided by NATO countries and the United States to complete their objectives of establishing a Fascist state to block our access to the Black Sea and the world. It is to stop this aggression that you are being called to service. I will now administer the oath that will make you honored members of the Russian Federation's Ground Forces of Liberation."

Petrov now repeated the oath with 200 others under Yoni's name, but could not escape the thought that it equally applied to him. "I, Yani Rabbivinovitz, solemnly swear allegiance to the Russian Federation, to the Motherland, and to the people. I swear to sacredly observe the Constitution of the Russian Federation, to strictly comply with the requirements of military regulations, orders of commanders and superiors. I swear to fulfill my military duty with dignity, to courageously defend the freedom, independence, and constitutional order of Russia, the people, and the Fatherland." To which Petrov added an additional, "I swear on my Stepfather's head and for the men I killed to do my best to make a freer, better Russia than I found. I swear."

Later that day, they would be herded back onto the train for their 17-hour trip to Vladivostok. Then he would really find out what being in the Russian Army was all about.

CHAPTER 7

IN THE ARMY OF LIBERATION

The raddling and banging of the cars awoke Petrov as the train pulled up to the station outside of the Admiral Stephan Osipovich Makarov base located on a plateau north of Vladivostok. Rina's head was lying on his shoulder, and he had to fight an impulse to kiss her. He was Yani now, and he had to play his part as a motivated Russian.

"Rina, wake up, we're here," he announced.

"Ohoo, Ohooo," she yawned. "I finally fell asleep. I'm so sorry if I bothered you on the last trip," Rina replied.

Once again, the cars were systematically emptied, and Starshina Kaplin escorted his platoon to the station's bathrooms and then into trucks for their transport deep into the base.

The crew passed rows of barracks, hangars, garages, workshops, bunkers, and warehouses to a series of wooden buildings dating from the last war. These were individual platoon barracks. The one where they stopped had an X-shaped wooden rack off to one side. Fresh piles of dirt indicated that this was newly installed.

"What's that?" Issak asked.

"I've seen pictures of them. It's a whipping rack." Yakov responded. "It is used as an intimidation. It's illegal to use them now."

"It works too," Yani thought as he felt an involuntary shiver run down his spine.

"Attention!" Kaplin barked. "Your officer, Comrade Lieutenant Androv Lebedev, will greet you in the morning. He has contacted me and said that his platoon must receive first honors among the 20 that are now in training. He has instructed me to see that you are the toughest, best-trained, and most capable of all. Is this understood? Reply!"

"Yes, I understand," came somewhat weekly from the platoon.

"Louder and together. You will reply like soldiers. Again," he ordered.

"Yes, I understand," came more forcefully from the Platoon's throats.

"Again! I want you to raddle the windows with the forcefulness of your reply," Kaplin demanded.

"YES, I UNDERSTAND," issued from the straining vocal cords.

"This is how you will answer if this question is asked," Kaplin responded. "If you do not understand, raise your hand. Comrade Lieutenant Lebedev is your new God, and I am St. Mikhail, his avenging angel. Your duty is to do whatever is asked of you, without hesitation, without question, and if it is your fate to take a bullet so that a Comrade can complete the mission, you might have a hero's death. Glory to the Russian Federation and the Army of Liberation. Repeat all together."

"Glory to …" resounded in a wave of sound that reverberated back from buildings across the square, and Fourth Rank Starshina Boris Kaplin felt satisfied with his progress. Partitions were put up to close off a sleeping area for the women and around two stalls that were reserved for them.

Well fed and tired from his journey, Yani gratefully put in the earplugs that were hanging in a bag by the door and retired to a lower bunk. Perhaps Kaplin did have real concerns about the well-being of his platoon, as shown by this thoughtful gesture. When he woke up with an urge to pee, he bumped his head on the steel frame of the bunk above him and had to remember where he was. Working his way back to the bathroom, he went to the metal trough and grabbed a pipe to steady himself as he peed.

******

Standing there, he closed his eyes and was transported to Rome, where he sat in the confession booth in the Basilica of St. John Lateran.

"Forgive me, Father, for I have sinned. It has been a year since my last confession. My vanity resulted in the death of my father and of three others who I killed to save my life. I want to do good but have done only evil."

"These are grievous sins and require great redemption. It will be your fate to redeem them just as Jesus died on the cross to redeem us. God will set you on a path. Be brave, be strong, and be steadfast in accomplishing His aims. As I have done, work to free the oppressed, serve your fellow men, and bring peace to a troubled world. Go now and sin no more."

Simultaneously relieved of a physical and spiritual burden, Yani returned to his bunk beside his sleeping comrades and fell into a deep sleep.

******

The next morning, Lt. Lebedev was driven in a GZ-67 whose four-cylinder engine wheezed, banged, and smoked as it arrived. The vehicle looked as if it had been drug across Mongolia, and perhaps it had sometimes during its life. With the platoon drawn up in front of the barracks, Lebedev was let out of the vehicle by the driver, and following him was a slim, hunched-over man dressed in a hooded white smock.

"Comrades, our country is in a time of crisis, and you have been elected to serve. I have been ordered to have you ready to go into combat in two months and given second and third-hand equipment to do it with because our first-line equipment is being sent to our valiant comrades at the front. We must use what we have to make you the best combat unit in this class. All of you were selected because you have different, but complementary, skills. You will be put to tasks that you can perform best, tested, and tested again until you can survive combat. It is late, but we will go to the mountains for winter training to harden your bodies against what you will face at the front.

"Krot, come forward. Tell these men what you do," Lebedev ordered.

"I have the honor of cleaning the sewers on this base," Krot replied.

"For how long will you do this job?" Lebedev asked.

"It will be my pleasure to serve in this manner for six years. I have served four, and have two more to go," Krot replied.

"Why were you given such a job?" Lebedev probed.

"To save my life. My comrades in the platoon would have killed me because I was reported as repeatedly speaking out against our Glorious

Leader Putin, who is once again putting Russia on the path to greatness." Krot spoke his lines as if he were performing on stage.

"Remove your smock and show yourself to the men," Lebedev ordered.

An involuntary gasp erupted as the platoon saw that Krot's face was scarred, his jaw displaced to the left, his back bent sharply forward, and when he turned around it was textured with a crosshatch of scars resulting from lashes from the knout with six leather strands attached to a meter-long pole.

"Present to the troops," Lebedev ordered.

As Knot passed in front of the platoon, he looked at each one of them with his single good eye as Lebedev continued, "Despite repeated warnings, this man continued to defile our leader and ultimately attempted to rape one of the women in his platoon, for which he was whipped nearly to death by his fellow platoon members. Each time, he was punished more severely than before, and he was to have been given 1000 lashes by members of the platoon before he was rescued. We will have a demonstration."

With these remarks, the driver took a man-sized manakin out of the back of the vehicle and chained it up to the whipping frame. Then he also retrieved a long cardboard box and placed it in front of the manakin.

"Starshina Kaplin, can you designate a person as Chief Whipper who can do justice to the instrument?" Lebedev asked.

"Yoni Rabbivinovitz, come forward," Kaplin ordered.

Having a better view of Yoni, Lebedev responded, "Yoni remove the knout from the box and get the feel of it. I want you to administer 20 strikes on the dummy."

Yoni felt the yew pole, which was checkered to provide a non-slip grip, and straightened the six strands of the knout. The knots had been soaked in brine to stiffen them, and tiny salt crystals still clung to the hard leather knots. Yoni separated his feet to allow a good swing as if he were chopping down a tree.

"This will be hot work. Take off your shirt," Lebedev ordered.

"You may begin striking the figure from the right shoulder to the left buttock for ten strikes and then reverse and do the same."

The weight of the long leather strands was balanced by the staff so that the knots on the strands carried enough momentum to dig into the manikin, with the result that pieces of white plastic and hard foam began to accumulate on the ground after each strike. Yani could feel the bite of the knots on the dummy and taste the salty sweat as it trickled into the corners of his mouth. He would not use this whip on a horse, much less on a man. When he had finished, the model had been very nearly quartered by the accumulated strikes of the whip, and hunks had been torn from the shoulders and hips.

As the driver took down the remains of the manakin, Lebedev asked, "These instruments need to be christened in blood. Do I have a volunteer to take two strikes? No. Then I will choose. You there with a smile on your face. Perhaps you think this is funny? Come up here."

Yakov came forward and stood before his Lieutenant.

"Yakov, what is your training?" Lebedev asked.

"I was training to be a psychologist with a dual major in higher mathematics before I was called up," Yakov replied.

"You volunteer to do this demonstration of your own free will?" Lebedev questioned.

"If it will further the objectives of liberating our oppressed countrymen in Ukraine, I will. I am ready," Yakov replied as bravely as he could muster as he started to fumble with the buttons of his shirt.

"I need this man's skills, and it would take him too long to recover from the demonstration. Do I have a volunteer to take his place?" Lebedev asked.

"I will," Sokolov answered.

Yoni gritted his teeth as he grasped his knout and prepared to swing at a person he didn't know well but had started to like. He did a silent prayer that he could judge the force of the strike sufficiently to draw blood with only two strikes, so as not to prolong the event. He drew back and paused, hoping that Lebedev would not order him to strike.

"Lightly ones from left to right and then from right to left. Blood must flow, or you will continue until it does. Driver, prepare the salt water," Lebedev directed.

Yoni swung at Sokolov's suspended form, taking care that the lines of the knout ran straight and did not touch the back of his head. He saw blood issue from the strike on Sokolov's shoulder and staining his trousers bright red. Quickly stepping to the other side, he administered the second blow with similar impact. He hoped that his job as Chief Whipper would never be repeated. Blood drawn from the strikes sprinkled him in the face, and its taste joined the salty sweat as he licked his lips. Now, not only was he a murderer, he was also a cannibal.

Sokolov responded with a violent flinch as he gripped the rawhide between his teeth on the first strike and again on the second. He collapsed and fainted when saltwater was thrown onto his back.

"The demonstration is concluded," Lebedev announced. "Take him back to the barracks and take care of him. He will receive medical treatment in the morning."

Yani carefully straightened out the lines of the knout and placed it back into its box. Then he helped Kaplan, Yakov, and Rina take Sokolov down from the rack and put him on a stretcher to take him back to the barracks.

After the men removed Sokolov's clothing, Rina used the first aid materials in the barracks to disinfect each of the bleeding wounds and put salve and bandages over them. Kaplan returned with an injection of morphine, which he administered.

"There will need to be a 24-hour watch on him until we can get him to the hospital. You will rotate in two-hour shifts. The dressings will need to be changed in four hours, and again in the morning. We will take care of our own, as much as we can," Kaplin ordered as he left the barracks.

"See, he's not so bad," Rina observed. "He's experienced, he knows what we are getting into. It would be wise to do what he says."

******

Yoni felt sweat run down his face as he topped the 10-meter log wall that he had just climbed as part of the obstacle course. Pausing for a second before descending the rope ladder hanging from the structure, he looked ahead to see Rina nimbly jumping through, over, and under the tires in the next obstacle field, which ended with fences that she easily vaulted over. She was leading the rest of the platoon.

"What a gal," he thought. "She's a gymnast too. She is going to beat all of us." Letting go of the ladder, he dropped into the sawdust pit, rushed through the tire obstacles, mounted the two fences, and found Rina hesitating in front of the water obstacle.

"On my back, quickly," Yoni shouted as he approached.

"I'm scared of the water. I can't swim," Rina responded with tears in her eyes.

"You can win this. You will. Get on my back, and we'll cross together," Yoni repeated. Another lady runner, Tova Abramovich was rapidly catching up. Yoni lifted Rina on his shoulders, stood, and began wading across the pond. The water rose to his armpits. He stumbled when his foot caught on a water lily, but he regained his footing. Somehow, the added weight seemed to be not so much a burden but a delight. "Was this the fulfillment of a caveman urge to carry off a woman?" he thought.

"Put me down," Rina asked when they had crossed the pond. She turned to him, hugged him, let go, and continued following the running path through the forest. She was like a wood nymph. Yoni stood entranced by the image until Tova slapped him on his back as she passed.

Not willing to let the women win everything, Yoni took up the chase. When they broke out of the woods, he saw a long, straight road with the finish line tower two kilometers ahead. Breathing deeply and cooled by the water, he picked up his pace and passed Tova, who was weakening on this long straightaway. Rina was still ahead by two hundred meters. He plowed ahead to cut the distance, but by the time the race was over, Rina still had a 50-meter lead.

Lieutenant Androv and Starshina Kaplan were in the tower at the finish line, taking notes on the runners as they passed. "That first one, who is she?" Androv asked.

"That is Rina Goldstein. She had some medical training at her village hospital and cleaned Sokolov's wounds. She is a village girl and used to hard work," Kaplan responded.

"Is Sokolov running?" Androv inquired.

"He insisted. We will have a chance to see what he is made of. If he finishes in spite of his injuries, he will have earned everyone's respect and would be a good candidate as a team leader," Kaplan suggested.

A loud series of voices from below interrupted their deliberations as Tova argued loudly that she had won because Yoni had helped Rina across the water obstacle, and both should be disqualified.

"Quiet!" Kaplin shouted down. "Whatever it is, this will be settled after the event is over."

"There is Sokolov. He's bleeding. Have someone take him and Rina to the barracks so she can treat him. They have shown us everything we need to see today."

"Who is that last one?" Androv asked.

"That is Issak, the watchmaker's son, who is a math whiz." Kaplin said.

"I need his intellect more than his body. Put him on added weight training and extra protein. He needs to be physically stronger than he is now," Androv ordered. "What was all that fuss about?"

"One of the women, Tova, claims that she won the event because Yoni helped Rina cross the water obstacle, and both ought to be disqualified. She says that Federation sports rules require this," Kaplin informed.

"Assure her that what she claims is true, but combat is not sport. It is survival. Helping each other is a skill that needs to be developed. In this event, cooperation as well as competitiveness are valued," Androv concluded.

******

"How does that feel?" Rina asked as she put hydrogen peroxide on Sokolov's bleeding scars and prepared the salve, gauze pads, and tape to cover the wounds.

"They sting and itch. I want to scratch them," the naked figure replied as he lay on his bunk.

"That's normal. The scabs are forming, which will protect the wounds, and they were abraded by your clothes. You must wear loose clothing and not scratch it. None are infected, which is good. I'll put numbing cream on them so you can sleep. How well do you know Yoni?" Rina asked.

"I know that he helped me down and brought me in, but I can't say I know him, or anyone here, yet. I have spoken to him a few times. He said he spent last winter as a woodcutter and came from north of the Amur. I like him. He seems friendly enough. Why do you ask?" Sokolov questioned.

"You are going to need some help bathing. He can help you. Let him. I want you to sleep on your stomach. I am going to put some pads over those places with just enough cover to keep you warm. Exposure to air will help you heal. I'll show him how to dress those bleeding spots. He seems sorry that he had to whip you and wants to help," Rina concluded.

"I won't lie. I had rather you doctor me than him, but if he'll help me get on my feet, I'll welcome his help. Is there something happening between you and him? You have spent a lot of time together," he gently probed.

"Maybe. I think there might be. I don't know. He seems to be very reluctant to tell me about himself, except that he is a Rabbi's son, and wasn't all that keen about it. He wanted to go into the Army instead, got his head shaved, and all of that," she admitted as she felt her face blush with embarrassment.

Rina felt relieved that Sokolov's face was turned away as he responded, "I had rather it be me, but he seems to be a nice-enough guy, if you want him."

Pushing himself up by his elbows, he turned to face Rina, but she turned away. "If things don't work out between you two, I'll be around. You are a very attractive woman. I've embarrassed you. I'm sorry. Enough of such talk," he said as he turned his head to look away.

******

"All this is from The Great War," Lebedev remarked to Starshina Kaplan as they looked at crates of arms and ammunition that had just arrived from the Vladivostok Arsenal.

"I usually start off with rifle training and would issue those first, then the submachine guns, and after we have decided, the heavy machine guns and mortar crews. Rabbivinovitz has experience in repairing these guns, and Sokolov is on light duty. I'll have them unpack the rifles tonight so that they can be issued before we go to the range tomorrow," Kaplan suggested.

There was only room for three men in the barracks armory. As fast as the guns could be cut from their paper and grease wrappings, Yoni pulled the bolts and inspected the firing pins. He found three where the pins or springs were broken.

"I'll take parts from guns with the worst barrels and repair these too," Yoni said.

"This is like a trip around the world," Pima Oelov remarked as he looked at the arsenal markings on the receivers. "Not only are there guns from Russian arsenals, but there are also some from Finland and even the US."

"The Finish ones have the reputation as being the better guns," Yoni replied. "Make sure that all the gun's parts are kept with that gun. They are not interchangeable, although they might look the same. Any that have mismatched parts we'll use as parts guns or try them out and remark them."

Androv was at the barracks when the rifles were issued the next morning as Starshina Kaplin logged in the serial numbers beside each person's name.

"Under present contingencies, these may be the guns that you use throughout your entire period of service. Care for them accordingly. I want you all to be able to hit the kill zone of a target at 300 meters. If your rifle seems to be inaccurate or not working, another will be issued to you," Androv informed the platoon.

While Kaplin was assembling the platoon, Androv remained. He drew his Nagant revolver and placed it on the desk in front of Yoni. "I was issued this and a box of ammunition, but it doesn't want to index properly. Can you fix it?"

Yoni took the gun, swung open the loading gate, and used the ejector to extract the long brass cartridges. Then he took the cylinder in his hand and pushed it back and forth into its locking position on the barrel.

"Comrade Lieutenant, the spring and hand are worn. I can fit new parts and have it back to you in a few hours."

"Fix it, and bring it out to the range. I want you there with some tools if the men have problems with their rifles," Androv ordered.

"Comrade Lieutenant, if I may speak?" Sokolov asked.

"What is it?" Androv responded.

"My father is the chief training officer at the Tula arsenal. For their trainees to pass, they must rebuild worn-out guns and arms of all types to shooting condition. Front-line commanders don't want those guns back, so he can send us practically anything we might like in about two weeks or have things like a new command vehicle ready for you in Moscow."

"That's excellent news. I'll make up a list, so we don't have to go into battle with our grandpa's guns. I know I'm going to want anti-drone and anti-tank equipment. Ask what he can get while we are still here so we can train with it. I will also want something with long-range sniping capabilities against vehicles and light armor," the Lieutenant added as he departed.

******

Back in the sleeping hall, Androv took Rina aside and told her, "Comrade Goldstein, for the second time, you have excelled by posting the best rifle shooting scores of the entire platoon. Your most valuable skills are not as a marksman, but as the team leader of our medical unit. However, you will be carrying a medical kit, and that rifle would impede your work. You will be issued a pistol. At times when drugs are scares or unavailable, it may be necessary…"

"I know. There is no need to say more, Comrade Lieutenant," Rina responded. "To end a life is sometimes the greatest mercy we can show."

"I have selected a strong man, Viktor Chao, to be your assistant. He will be issued a SKS, which is a smaller rifle that you should also train with. It will fit you better and has less recoil. The good ones can be very accurate out to 300 meters. You two should start training together. If this doesn't work out, let me know," Androv assured Rina, who was showing signs of doubt.

The next day at the range, the platoon was introduced to the PPSh-41 submachine gun with its 71-round drum magazines and the SKS 7.62x39 with its short rifle round and 10-round capacity. Chao and Rina were paired together and listened to Lieutenant Androv describe the guns.

"If we get into trench combat, the shorter submachine gun and SKS are useful for close-range combat. The submachine gun, shooting the pistol cartridge can spray an area very quickly when shot from the hip and serve to suppress fire even when making an assault on a trench. The SKS, with its more powerful cartridge and greater accuracy, is useful for penetrating some body armor or taking shots at the limbs or head to disable an enemy. The objective is to overwhelm the enemy with firepower as quickly as possible and move on. We may get some AK-47s, but it is arguable if these are more efficient for close-range fighting," Androv informed.

Waiting between relays, Rina had the chance to talk to Chao, "Where are you from, and how did you get here?" Rina asked.

"I had been convicted of drug dealing and murder and sent to the Polar Wolf penal colony in Kharp. I was given the choice of coming to fight or a life sentence. I chose to join up with the understanding that if I fought well, I could be set free. I arrived too late for the first levy and was sent to this unit instead," Chao said in an unapologetic voice.

"You did some bad things?" Rina probed.

"Yes, particularly against women and young men who would not cooperate with what my bosses wanted them to do. There is no need to tell you about them. I did what I was paid to do. It was a job. A terrible job, but a job, nonetheless. I sometimes find myself wanting to do those things now. I have my temptations, but Kitten, I don't want to wind up like Krot," Chao responded.

******

"Don't ever call me that," Rina rebuffed. "You may call me Nurse, but nothing else. This will be a professional relationship, or you'll go back to prison."

Yoni quickly found Lieutenant Androv and gave him the pistol. "Comrade Lieutenant, here is your revolver. I have fixed it. All the other parts were good, and there is no reason it should not serve you well.

They built good guns at Tula." Yoni said as they walked to a firing position on the 25-meter range.

Androv loaded the gun and fired at the silhouette target. Shooting double action and single action, he kept all the shots in the chest area.

"That's good, sir, considering the ammunition was made in 1943. With a rest and good ammo, I suspect that the gun will shoot 2-centimeter groups at that range," Yoni remarked as he thought, "That gun is most likely going to be used against one of us, and maybe me."

******

If conditions in the barracks were rough, they were even more confined in the winter training area, where each platoon was housed in a yurt-type tent with a wood stove in the center. Some blankets were used to partition off an area for the four women and a portion of the multi-stalled communal out-house reserved for them.

A separate tent contained racks for the guns to prevent them from collecting condensation and freezing when exposed to below-zero temperatures. The surrounding mountains still had snow, and patches remained on the northern slopes and in shaded areas around the camp. Donning snowshoes or skis, they left each morning to practice on the slopes and shoot at a variety of targets.

At a range of pop-up targets, Rina, Chao, and Yoni were shooting together. "I'll take those that are farthest away, Chao you shoot those at mid-range, and Rina you take the close ones with your Tokarev," Yoni suggested.

"Who are you to be giving me orders?" Chao demanded.

Unsure how to reply, Yoni hesitated, but Rina responded, "He is my friend. Do what he says."

"So, boss lady, that is how it is? Is it?" Chao gruffly replied.

"Yes, that is how it is. If you cause any harm to come to her, I will kill you. Don't doubt that," Yoni responded.

"Quit," Rina ordered. "If we are all going to get through this thing alive, we've got to get along. You two shake hands and pay attention. If we all score well, we will be able to get more of what we want."

"Ready," came Kaplin's voice over the loudspeaker. "Fire."

The first target broke through the snow at 30 meters, and Rina hit it with a shot from her pistol. The next was at 500 meters, and Yoni got that one with his rifle. This was quickly followed by another at 200 meters, which Chao shot with the SKS. More targets came in rapid sequence as some were raised again and others appeared accompanied by a rising crescendo of small arms fire from all along the line. The exercise continued for half an hour, during which each shooter had to reload or change magazines.

"Cease fire," Kaplin ordered. "Each group count to your remaining ammunition and report that to the tower."

Assembling the unit, Androv addressed the platoon. "This exercise was to teach you how to address different targets at different ranges with different weapons while using as little ammunition as possible. Reloading takes time, and that is when you are most likely to be attacked by an enemy. The winner of this exercise was the team consisting of Rina, Chao, and Yoni. You all shot significantly better than average. You will be allowed to go to the spa tonight and relax."

Although the troop was to have only four hours at the spa, each sought to make the most out of it. Yoni enjoyed a soak in the waters, which helped relax his tired muscles. Issak joined him along with Chao and most of the other men. Sokolov went straight to the massage table, where he was hand bathed and had his wounds treated. The wood frame and Nordic theme of the spa were complemented by large windows where the guests could see the snowy mountains, admire the huge trees in the forest, and relax with a herbal tea before loading up for the trip back to the camp.

The four women in the platoon, Rina, Tova, Anya Kaganovich, and Fatima Safarova had their first opportunity to talk among themselves without having men nearby.

"Anya, why did you join the army? I did because I did not want to marry the old man that the matchmaker picked out for me. Was it something similar for you?" Rina asked.

"Yes and no. I was accused of sleeping around, which I did, and that spoiled everything for me. I had to leave. With no particular skills, the Army was the only option for me," Anya responded.

"And you, Fatima? Rina inquired.

"There was another woman who was jealous of me because I had gone to school, and she had not. She accused me of stealing something. She kept saying that I had taken this or that. She kept the community in such turmoil that I had to leave. I could not get out of the country, and the Army was my best choice. I was told that I would be a translator, but was assigned to this combat unit," Fatima replied as she ran her fingers through her black hair.

"So you are not a Muslim?" Tova questioned.

"I believe in many Muslim principles, but not with the strict practices of the faith," Fatima revealed.

"What do you all think of the men in the platoon?" Tova asked.

"I like Yoni," Rina replied. "I've talked to him and think that he is a nice, helpful, man. I don't know if it is going anywhere, but we could maybe do something together."

"I think that Sokolov might be the one for me. He's got something on the ball, so to speak. He also has connections and money. You've seen him, Rina, what do you think?" Tova queried.

"As a physical specimen, he is a handsome guy with all the equipment that you might want. That's about all I know," Rina replied.

"I don't want any of them," Fatima replied. After those men drove me out of my village, I hate them all. I want nothing to do with men, except to have them in my rifle sights," Fatima affirmed.

"I'm ambivalent towards them all. I can't say I have any particular favorites. I'll take them or leave them, I guess," Anya responded.

The blowing of the bus's horn ended their conversation, and they returned to barracks to prepare for their cross-continental trip to Moscow.

CHAPTER 8
ACROSS RUSSIA

The forty-car train shuttered as it pulled into Yekaterinburg. The armored troop-transport cars were interspersed among the flat-bed cars loaded with tanks, dozers, artillery pieces, and lumber. "The Vl80 electric locomotive was thirsty again," Yoni thought. He knew he was. When they skirted Lake Baikal, the train had taken on meals of poached golomyanka whose buttery oil-rich flavor was particularly satisfying. It had been served with a relish made of chopped cucumbers, green peppers, and carrots along with small loaves of crusty sourdough bread, which Yoni used to sop up the tasty sauce.

"This is the best fish that I have ever had," Yoni remarked to Rina, who was sitting beside him. "We could never afford it in our village. We had carp, sturgeon, and salmon, but this is even better."

"Would anyone like tea?" Issak asked. "I'll get it."

"Beer would be better," Sokolov volunteered. "I bet they have plenty of that in the officer's car."

"If we're dreaming, what about a nice white Georgian wine like Rkatsiteli, with its citrus flavor and sparkle. Looking through the bars on the windows, I could see two cases of it at the station. Our officers are eating well," Chan speculated.

"I'm sure our glorious leader would approve," Issak intoned.

Yoni raised his fingers to his lips and whispered to Issac, "That tongue of yours is going to get you whipped yet. Anyone in this car could turn you in. You're my friend. I don't want to do it, but I would have to if I were ordered to administer punishment."

"As one who has felt the bite of that whip, I assure you that you would not like it," Sokolov added.

With a full belly and Rina's head resting on his shoulder, Yoni was lulled to sleep by the steady, clank, clank, clank of the train as it made its way. He experienced a look at the real Russia, its power, its hopes, its history, and its desperation compared to the propaganda that everyone had been fed since childhood.

In his mind, he retraced the journey. Starting at Vladivostok, there were dense forests, and a track that was often supported by bridges and trestles that crossed swift-flowing streams and rivers with sparse and infrequent settlements clinging to the track like a lifeline. In about a day of travel, the topography flattened out as they broke out into the grasslands of the Siberian plains, peopled now by herdsmen raising sheep, goats, horses, and pigs. Periodically, there were pens and animal loading ramps where trains stopped each spring to load their live cargo. The smell of urine and animal dung told those within the cars that another loading dock had been passed.

The air cleared as the land dried in Southern Siberia, and more dust was churned up by the tumbleweed rolling and catching on the fences. The dust coming into the cars was flavored with the bitter smell of wormwood, which became more intense as the sun heated the desert. As the Urals were approached, settlements became more numerous, surrounded by fields of rye, barley, and hops stretching towards the horizon.

******

Lieutenant Androv had asked Starshina Kaplin to join him to assist in completing a report on the status of his platoon that he had to turn in when he arrived in Ukraine.

"Starshina Kaplin, please give me the most honest assessment that you can of the platoon. I need to know how well you think the training went and the status of our weapons," Androv asked.

"The platoon will fight to protect their fellow members and themselves. I do not think that they are particularly motivated to fight in Ukraine or anywhere else. The exceptions seem to be Yoni, who fixed your revolver, Sokolov who arranged for us to get the anti-tank drone system-launcher, and Fatima who is just ready to kill any man because she hates all men," Kaplin replied.

"When we change trains in Moscow, I'm going to add a conference car and want to talk to all the corporals. I want you to be there too. How are the weapons crews?" Androv queried.

"We did receive the anti-light-vehicle rifle. It takes a three-person crew to operate it effectively. Fatima has been training with it. With day or night sights, it can hit a vehicle at over 1,000 meters. That new muzzle break not only hides flash but is also an effective silencer."

"Sokolov did well with the time he had with the drone and the anti-tank rocket. I would advise that we let him continue to lead that unit."

"Issak is as close to a 'natural' as I have ever seen with the mortar crew. He can calculate the angles in his head and place the shells exactly where they are needed."

"Yoni distinguished himself not only as an armorer but also on the heavy machine gun. He has a good eye for tactical deployment and sufficient woods knowledge to properly set up a position and conceal the gun. He follows instructions well and has served as an example for the entire platoon. Despite being the designated 'Whipper,' everyone in the platoon respects him. If anything happened to me, I would suggest that he be my replacement," Kaplan concluded.

******

After sitting on the hard benches for four days, everyone was delighted when they were ordered off the train, given stretching exercises, and marched to a mess hall for dinner while the train was being reconstituted for their final two-day trip to the front. Carloads of ammunition, foodstuffs, drones, and communication equipment were being added, along with additional tanks for their mechanized units. Two open-topped cars bristling with machine guns were added to ward off possible drone attacks on the final leg of their journey.

"I never liked exercises, but I'll admit that after four days of sitting on those wooden benches, it felt good to move around again. It also feels good to be eating off real dishes and tableware, instead of out of boxes," Issak opined.

"Did you see the sailing boats on the Moskva River when we crossed at Kolomna? My dad and I sometimes sailed my Amurisky when I was a boy. It would be nice to rent a boat and sail like those people from Moscow were doing," Yoni offered.

"Fat chance, they would never let us off this base. They are too eager to get us to the battlefield, wherever that is," Issak responded.

"Enjoy your Chicken Kiev and shut up," Yoni responded as he cut another slice of his chicken breast, and the combined odors of dill and parsley filled his nostrils as his teeth enjoyed the satisfying crunch of the egg-battered exterior. The combination of rye bread, glazed carrots, peas, and mashed potatoes completed the meal, which was washed down with glasses of milk, followed by tea and a mixed plate of sweet pastries, of which the honey-glazed pryanik with its gingerbread core was his favorite.

"I like those too, but the baker would only make them at Christmas. They were always special to me," Rina added as they enjoyed their tea for a few minutes before they resumed their trip.

As the platoon formed up on the platform prior to resuming their journey, a commotion occurred in another platoon further down on the platform. Overheard were shouts of "I won't go. I'd rather die."

Before the train resumed its journey, Kaplin gathered Yoni, Rina, Sokolov, Issak, and Fatima and took them to the special conference car that Lieutenant Ankarov had requested.

"Please be seated," Ankarov said as he gestured for them to sit at the table. "I must turn in a report on the combat readiness of this platoon. Thanks to the efforts of Sokolov's father, we have a new combat vehicle, more anti-tank drones, and have been resupplied with ammunition. What I need to hear from you is about your team's readiness for combat. Yoni, you first."

"Comrade Lieutenant, we are ready to serve the Fatherland. I've had a chance to test the machine gun out to 3,000 meters, and my team can get the gun into an effective position and use it within a few minutes. Mechanically, the gun is old, but it is solid. With the new mount, I can put it on your vehicle or deploy it separately."

"Very good. Sokolov," Ankarov ordered.

"Comrade Lieutenant, the new command vehicle is on the train. The BMP-3 has a driver, gunner, and loader who will be joining our platoon. It has a 100mm gun that can shoot conventional shells and anti-tank guided missiles, a 30mm auto-cannon, and a 7.62 machine gun. You haven't had the opportunity to train on this machine or its guns. It can also carry eight platoon members. I think that at least a week's training on this machine would be necessary to get the most out of it.

"My father had a special gun made up for you to shoot the 12.7X108 armor-piercing round with a modified barrel from the Kord machine gun and a combined silencer and flash hider on a tripod mount. It is very accurate and comes with a compensated day-time sight and a thermal sight for night use. Its effective range against small vehicles is out to 2,000 meters. It would be best served by a gunner, loader, and ammo carrier/spotter. It should be concealed on some high point to take advantage of its range and silent operation. Any enemy would have difficulty in determining where the shot originated. Fatima has been designated team leader, and can give you her report," Sokolov concluded.

"Thank you and thank your father for the delivery of our command vehicle. I also agree with your assessment that I need time to master the MBP-3 and all its systems. Fatima, what is your opinion of the rifle?" Ankarov asked.

"Comrade Lieutenant, my team can set up, conceal, and fire the rifle in five minutes. We are ready to engage any enemy of the Federation," Fatima offered.

"Thank you all for your reports. I will request that we be assigned to a support area for a week before we go to the front. I have a demonstration to do at the next stop, after which you may return to your car. When we stop, you men will form up and stand behind me. Grab those hammers and bent pieces of reinforcing rod as you leave," Ankarov ordered.

******

The train stopped at a siding surrounded by fields of emerging wheat. After the company had been assembled, three men drug a naked man out into the field and held him upright as a voice over the loudspeaker spoke, "You have been tried and convicted of desertion, refusal to obey orders, and defaming our leader. For these crimes, you will be cast out of the company and left to the vultures and animals to feed on while you are yet alive. Administer the punishment."

Yoni saw the fear in the man's eyes as he helped push him to the ground and pounded the sharpened U-shaped rebar stakes around his wrist deep into the black soil. When they had finished, Ankarov took his pistol and fired a single shot through the gagged man's abdomen. The jaws opened as if to scream, but no sound emerged. One of the escorts took a plastic bag containing his tongue and pored it and honey over the man's body.

After the shot, Ankarov holstered his revolver and turned to the assembled company. He shouted, "Long live the Russian Federation and the honor of The Army of Liberation," and motioned with his arms for the men to repeat the cheer. After three repetitions, the men filed back into their cars to continue their journey to Crimea.

No one in Petrov's car was in the mood to talk as the cities, towns, and fields passed by on their journey south. The train passed through Kursk and stopped on the outskirts of Belgorod, where a bustling camp had been established in the basins of the Donets River, where dams on the Oskol and Seversky rivers provided abundant water. Replacing the once lush forests were scattered orchards of apples, pears, cherries, and plums around the rivers. Yoni salivated as he saw the trees hanging heavy with fruit, as he imagined eating a chilled Kisel filled with crushed cherries and plums, or maybe there would even be Varenye, a preserve, made of mixed fruits to spread over his rye bread. He used these thoughts to displace the horror of what he had done.

******

Some of the camp's buildings were made of insulated panels with preset windows and doors, which had already experienced a winter, while rows of tents and sometimes improvised wooden, tin, and canvas structures dominated the areas designated for units in transit. Disembarking from the train, Ankarov's platoon marched to their tents, where their unit designation was pinned to a pole like a street sign. None had to be encouraged to go to sleep on a bed that wasn't moving.

At the morning formation, Ankarov announced, "We are to be posted in a forward guard position where we will dig in just as if it were on the front line. Unfortunately, this area is too populated for us to fire our weapons. You will have your ammunition with you, but do not load or fire unless ordered."

The first night in their new trenches passed uneventfully. The rich, black soil dug softly and easily, and planks and boards were needed to brace up the sides and support the roofs of the dugouts that were to be used for sleeping. The BMP-3 was sunk into a depression to provide protective fire and communications.

Lieutenant Ankarov was awakened at about 2:00 AM by Starshina Kaplin, "Sir. Come see. Something is happening ahead of us."

"What, What?" Ankarov groggily replied.

"There is artillery fire and lights just over the horizon. I think the Ukrainians are coming," Kaplin shouted.

"Nonsense, we are miles from the front; it must be some unit's night exercises. I can't imagine why they can shoot their guns, and we can't. I'll file a complaint tomorrow. Now that I'm awake, I'm going to check the sentries," Ankarov replied.

"If you say so, sir, I thought you needed to know," Kaplin said as Ankarov left the vehicle.

CHAPTER 9

COMBAT

"What do you think of our Lieutenant?" Zuar Umarov asked Sergei Volkov and Nick Mikhailov after Kaplin and Ankarov left the BPM-3.

"I just load the gun. What do I know?" Sergei replied. "I just hope he doesn't get us all killed."

"I think he is a hotshot young officer trying to make a name for himself. Something is happening out there, but the radio is so messed up that I can't pick up anything. Either we are in a period of high sunspot activity, or we are being jammed. I can't tell which."

"If we do have to fight, how much live ammo do we have?" Zuar asked?

"We have a full load for the machine gun, just smoke for the 30 mm, and just three anti-personnel rounds for the main gun. The anti-tank rounds and rockets are all being shipped to the front," Nick replied.

"I'll tell the Lieutenant when he returns," Zuar offered.

"What for? Even if we sent for ammo, it would be midday before we could get it," Nick argued. "No one is going to answer such a request until they've had their tea and crumpets, as the English might say. That would only get the Lieutenant in trouble for waking everyone up over nothing."

When he returned from checking the positions, Androf asked, "Is there anything on the radio?"

Comrade Lieutenant, "Only static. I can't pick up anything," Nick replied.

"It's cloudy and overcast. Maybe rain later. I can't see the sky. If this stuff turns to mud, will we be able to move?" Ankarov asked.

"We can install wider tracks for snow, but what we have on now are road treads. If it gets too wet, we could be stuck in his hole," Zuar responded.

"I'll have the men cut some poles and brush to put under the tracks in the morning. In the meantime, shut down and get some sleep. We'll see if I can send in the Morning Report at 9:00 A.M.," Ankarov concluded as he climbed into his hammock.

In his forward position in a foxhole, Pavel Bogdanovich was having a restless night digging and filling sandbags with the soil to put around his position. Looking as far as he could to the south, the line of lights appeared to be coming closer.

Earlier that evening, he had been visited by Ankarov.

"Halt and identify yourself," Pavel ordered as he heard footsteps approaching.

"Lieutenant Ankarov, Password 'gloriosa'," he answered.

"Advance and be recognized," Pavel said as he strained to see the lieutenant.

"Glad to see you, sir. Something is going on. There are flashes of light bouncing off the clouds. I can't tell if it's lightning or maybe a convoy advancing along a road in the storm," Pavel reported.

Taking out his binoculars, Ankarov searched the horizon, but his lenses only collected water droplets.

"I can't make out anything in this rain. We haven't been notified of any enemy activity. It must be some weather phenomenon. When you see what is going on, report it on the land line. All the radios are down," Ankarov concluded.

"Yes, sir," Pavel assented.

"In two hours, I will send someone to relieve you," Ankarov offered.

"Thank you, sir," Pavel responded, although he was not all that sure that one wet hole in the ground was better than any other. At least he would not be alone.

Yoni hauled up a pale of rations when he went to relieve Pavel. The only way he knew for sure where he was going was by holding the communication wire in his hands as his feet felt their way towards the forward position.

"Yoni, Glad to see you. I'm so wet and cold that I can hardly move," Pavel stammered as his teeth clanked like castanets.

Yoni gave Pavel three energy bars and told him to follow the wire back to the BPM-3 command vehicle, where he could find dry clothes and warm up.

"This may be my chance," Yoni thought. "If the Ukrainians are advancing, I can surrender to them. For the moment, we watch and wait."

He suddenly heard a buzzing noise above the sound of the wind. "That's a drone. Got to be. Theirs' or ours?" he postulated.

The drone hesitated, but then proceeded towards Kursk and would pass over their camp. If he didn't call it in, maybe the rest of the platoon would not notice. He could always say that he didn't see it. It had not attacked him, but with infrared, it may have spotted him.

The sound of a single vehicle was what he heard next. The driver barreling down the road with only his shielded combat lights on could see no better than he.

"Stop. Stop and be recognized," Yoni shouted. There was no immediate response, so Yoni fired a shot in the air and repeated the command. The driver hit the brakes and skidded until a wheel hit Yoni's line of sandbags, which flipped the truck, ejected the driver, and rolled over him.

"Tanks, scores of them. Right behind me. Got to warn people," the driver gasped with blood gurgling from his crushed rib cage.

"I'll take care of it. You did good," Yoni assured the dying man as he coughed his last breath.

Searching through the man's bag, he found a set of over whites from which he cut a white rectangle to fix to his bayonet.

A few minutes later, the rumble and clank of tank treads on the asphalt road became apparent, and Yoni stood in the middle of the road with his unloaded gun, frantically waving the flag in front of the first tank.

"Do you wish to surrender?" a megaphoned voice asked from the lead Abrams tank.

"Yes. I want to join you. There is a platoon ahead of you. If you can surround them, I think I can get them to surrender," Yoni offered.

Two men appeared who took his rifle, pistol, grenades, and knife before hoisting him up on the front of the tank where he could talk to the commander.

"They have dug trenches in front of the village and have a new BPM-3. I did not see any anti-tank missiles, but they may have some anti-tank ammo. We were supposed to still be in training. This is a command carrier, and is equipped with the latest radios and scanning equipment," Yoni explained.

"That would be quite a prize even if it were damaged. I'll go for it," Group Commander Volodymyr said. While approaching the town, he spread his lighter weight, tracked vehicles on field roads so as daylight approached, all anyone in the town would see would be gun muzzles pointed in their direction.

"You are surrounded. Surrender." Volodymyr's voice echoed across the platoon's entrenchments.

Throwing himself out of his hammock, Lieutenant Ankarov tried to comprehend what he was hearing. "Was this part of an exercise or was it real?" he questioned.

He opened the rear door, and in the early daylight, he could see tanks and other vehicles flying the Ukrainian flag all around them.

A single shell exploded in a nearby field to apparently emphasize the point. Approaching him was an armored pick-up truck with a machine gun mounted over its cab and a large Ukrainian flag flying from its fender.

"I'm going out to talk to their commander. Take the hammocks down and gather anything else that we can put under the treads. Get the 30mm ready to fire all the smoke we've got. I am going to try to break out of here. They mustn't capture this vehicle. If I am killed, Starshina Kaplin, you take command and see that this vehicle is destroyed. And especially the code books," Ankarov directed.

"I do not think so, Comrade Lieutenant," Chao said as he pointed his Makarov pistol at Ankarov.

"You'll be hanged for this," Ankarov shouted.

"I'll be hanged anyway. What does it matter? I, all of us, would rather live and be exchanged than die here for nothing. What you are suggesting would get us shot like rats," Chao added.

Yoni's voice came over the megaphone, "Comrades, this is Yoni. I have been assured by the commander that if you surrender, you will be treated well. You will be given the option of going to another country or being held until the next prisoner exchange can be arranged. I believe him, don't throw your lives away in this mudhole."

From their elevated point of concealment, Rina, Tova, and Fatima witnessed what was going on. "That traitor, Yoni, is with those Ukrainians. He needs to be killed."

"I'll take him out with this," Fatima suggested.

"No. Save that. It should be Rina who kills him. Otherwise, she will be thought to be involved in this treachery," Tova countered.

"I want to. He lied to me about everything. I'll get closer with my SKS and shoot him. Should I fail, then you can have him. Have them all," Rina replied, trying to keep her voice firm and determined. She was glad to have the rain hide the tears running down her cheeks.

Slipping quietly down towards the camp, she used blueberry shrubs and orchard trees for cover as she approached. Bracing herself behind a large pomegranate tree, she could smell the fruit hanging heavily from the branches.

"He's there. In the truck. I'll wait until he gets out," She thought. Satisfied that she had the target identified, she concealed herself as well as she could with fallen branches and checked the rifle to make sure the barrel was clear. Waiting for a thunderclap, she loaded it, checked the safety, and waited. She felt confident she could make the shot.

******

"Lieutenant, time is short. Make up your mind," Surrender us or die."

"Sokolov, Kaplin, get that gun!" Ankarov shouted.

As the two men started to move, Sergei, Nick, and Zuar grabbed them and held them down. Chao calmly raised the pistol and, looking Ankarov in the eye, shot him through the heart. The men released Kaplin, and he went to his dying Lieutenant's side in time to hear, "Destroy the codes and radio."

"We must destroy the codes and radio. They can't have those," Kaplin demanded.

"Those are worth a lot of money, more than you are Starshina," Chao said as he shot Kaplin in the forehead, blowing brains and blood out of the back of his skull.

"None of us can ever go back," Sokolov stated. "If there is money, then it must be shared."

"Equal shares for everyone, including me, we will prosper together or hang together. Agreed?" Chao questioned.

"Very well, it seems that you all want to live. Put your guns, grenades, and knives on the floor. When I drop the rear hatch, walk out with your hands up, and form up behind me," Chao ordered.

As they walked out, the sound of a pin being pulled from a grenade is heard, followed by the sound of it striking the floor and rolling towards the control panel.

"Grenade. Run!" Issak shouted as the group dispersed in an attempt to get out of the blast area. The grenade exploded, igniting the smoke canisters for the 30mm. This caused billows of black smoke to rise from the BPM-3, and heated the practice rounds to the point of explosion.

Partly concealed by the smoke, Sokolov ran through the line of troops in an attempt to make his way towards Kursk. He is challenged by a tank gunner and brought down by three rounds from a burst from the tank's machine gun.

Hearing the sequential detonations of the ammunition on the troop carrier, Volodymyr told Yoni, "I'll send a team to look over it later. There is not going to be much left. You stay with my Starshina and guards. There will be a truck to take you to Kiev. I am going to push on towards Kursk. Good luck," With these parting words, the commander rallied his tanks and vehicles and departed.

As the wind drifted the smoke away, Rina saw Yoni pause as he spoke to Issak, "You can get away now if you want…"

Yoni felt a burn in his right shoulder and fell to the ground.

Issak helped Yoni down into a trench while the Starshina rallied his guards to go after the sniper.

Satisfied that she had done what she intended to do, Rina snuck away from the battle zone to find some intact Russian unit.

******

The prisoner's truck arrived. Most of the prisoners were loaded into the personnel transporter with its three rows of benches. Yoni was in a large-cab pick-up stretched across the back seat. Issak's bandages were holding, and the morphine a medic had given him helped. He thought of the irony that once more he was entering a new phase in his life, wounded and helpless.

With the driver behind the wheel and Issak in the middle, and Chao in the window seat, a chatter was going on in the front seat. Chao was mad that his payday had been ruined, and his reward lost for turning in the command vehicle.

******

"Forty-four clicks up and three right windage," Fatima said as she dialed the gun barrel up to engage the pick-up at 1200 meters. Taking a breath, she pressed the fire button and quickly worked the bolt to chamber another round.

The impact of the bullet was felt as it penetrated the roof, passed over Issak's head, and blew a 14cm hole in the front windshield.

"That must be Fatima." Get down.

The next round exploded a rubber fragment from a rear tire, and although the vehicle now had a jarring thump with every revolution, the driver was able to control the wheel and proceed down the road.

"We must be out of range now," Chao said as Fatima's third shot came through the back of the vehicle, struck him in the throat, nearly separating Chao's head from his body. For a time, a scrap of skin held the head, which banged against the outside of the door until it fell into the roadway.

******

Exhaustion, loss of blood, fatigue, and the painkiller that he had been given finally conspired to put Yoni into a deep sleep. He vaguely remembered being put on a gurney and rushed down white hospital hallways, bathed, operated on, and put into a ward bed with other wounded. He was fortunate that the round had cleanly penetrated his shoulder, not hit a lung. The doctor assured him that he would be back to normal in three months.

Yoni asked if anyone else from the platoon was in the hospital.

Looking at his clipboard, the doctor replied. "There is another who was brought in at the same time that you were. He is a Corporal Sokolov with gunshot wounds to his face, arm, and leg. It's painful for him to talk, but you both are going to be here for several days. You will be able to visit him when you have regained enough strength to walk."

The next day, orderlies had Yoni walking with a cane and supported him on both sides as he made his way down the hall and back to his bed. He passed Sokolov's bed and waved. Sokolov responded by raising his good hand and slowly lowering it again. A few days later, as both grew stronger, Yoni was able to walk alone, and Sokolov motioned him over.

With casts on two limbs and a bandage over half of his face, Sokolov was unable to communicate as strongly as he wanted to, but he could now be understood.

"Voice therapy," Sokolov told Yoni. "They want me to talk as much as possible to strengthen my jaw muscles. I can only eat baby food now. Disgusting stuff."

"I had injuries to my arms and leg, like when I was attacked by that bear. I don't know if those were any better than what you've got," Yoni replied.

"What happened to Chao?" Sokolov asked.

"Well, you know he was all about the money he could get by selling the Command Vehicle and codes, he lost his head over it. Fatima got him with her rifle and blew his head off. As we were getting away, it bounced on the truck door for some time, held by a scrap of skin. It is out there in a ditch somewhere."

The poietic justice of Chao being shot by a woman and literally losing his head amused Sokolov to where he went into convulsive laughter, to the point where a nurse came and made Yoni leave.

Later, with Yoni now much more mobile and Sokolov in a wheelchair, Yoni was able to wheel Sokolov outside to a spot where they could talk more privately.

"I am to be exchanged tomorrow," Sokolov said. "I am to be given a metal for keeping the command vehicle and codes out of enemy hands. I'll be given a new assignment with the FSV."

"You. You were the mole!" Yoni exclaimed.

"Yes, I was and am. Yoni, we have become friends, but my next duty will be to track all the mutineers down and put them on trial or kill them. That includes you. You want to defect, you aided the enemy, you betrayed Mother Russia. Run fast and hard Yoni, the FSV's reach is long, and we don't quit. I promise that if I do it, your end will be personal and swift. Wheel me back inside," Sokolov concluded.

No more was said. The pair made their departures in silence under somber and threatening skies.

CHAPTER 10

THE CIA

"Corporal Rabbivinovitz, I am Captain Cheriolisky with the Ukrainian Intelligence Service, and I understand that you want to join our cause? Is this correct?" the officer asked.

Yoni raised himself on his good elbow so that he had a better look at a robustly built uniformed man with a silver and gilt-mounted swagger stick tucked under his right arm.

"Yes, sir. I do. I want to help defeat Putin's objective of becoming an imperial Russia, and violating our constitution and sworn duty," Yoni responded.

"Your documents say that you were born in Khabarovsk, the son of a Rabbi, and responded to a call to service. Is this correct?"

"Only partly. It is true that I was born in Khabarovsk to a Jewish couple, but as a baby, I was sold to an Orthodox family in a village on the Buria River and raised by them. My stepfather, a dissident, fought to keep me from being taken. They killed him, and I killed a Commissar and two troopers to escape. I spent the winter trapping. I was attacked by a bear, burned in my sleeping bag when I fired a pistol, and shot myself in the foot. With the help of a Nanai family, my wounds were healed. I sold my furs and an ivory tusk to a Chinese Tong leader named Wei, who put me under his protection. By accident, I met my twin brother who had induction papers. With the help of my father, Moshi, I substituted for him, went through training, and traveled with my platoon here. I was put in a forward position alone. I did not report a recon drone and did not notify anyone when a messenger's vehicle crashed in a storm. I convinced the Ukrainian commander, Volodymyr, that I could get my platoon to surrender and let him capture a new BPM-3 Command Transport with all the new communication and detection equipment.

"Unknown to me, a convicted murderer named Chao had already killed Lieutenant Ankarov and Starshina Kaplin. Chao was surrendering the BPM-3 when Corporal Sokolov threw a grenade inside and destroyed the vehicle. Then my girlfriend, Corporal Rina, shot me in the shoulder. Chao was killed when we were driving away by Corporal Fatima, who shot his head off with a 15 mm machine gun round fired from a special long-range rifle.

"Corporal Sokolov told me earlier today that he was the FSV's mole in the platoon and that his first duty was to bring all the platoon members to trial, or if he could not, he would kill us all. He is smart, resourceful, and clever. He and the three women will receive metals, and then he will start looking for us," Yoni concluded.

"And you expect me to believe all that?"

"Nurse. Nurse. Down here. Undress this man, I need to look at his wounds." Cheriolisky ordered.

The head nurse appeared and asked, "What is this about? It's not time for a bandage change."

"This man has just told me a fantastic story; I need to know if it is true," Cheriolisky said.

"There are pictures in his file," she said as she pulled a clipboard from the end of the bed and quickly turned through the pages.

"See, here is the gunshot wound through the shoulder, and here is a picture of his face when we were picking out the glass fragments. Thankfully, his eye was not hit, although there may be some reaction. He also has old scars from burns on his hands, a healed bullet scar in his right foot, and burn scars on his hands and fingers. Those you can look at yourself," she said as she turned and departed, leaving Cheriolisky to his own investigations.

"Very well. Let me see your hands and feet."

Yoni offered him his left hand and stuck his foot out from beneath the sheets. Cheriolisky had to move to the other side of the bed to see Yoni's right hand, which he looked at and annotated.

"Either you are the most accomplished storyteller that I have ever heard, or what you are telling me is true. No one could have made up such a fantastic story. If this agent and the women are to get awards, there will be Pravda stories about it. It will take a few days to check things out. In the meantime, a guard will be with you at all times with instructions to kill you, should you attempt to escape."

"Comrade Captain, I did not come all the way across Siberia and most of Russia to run away. Put me wherever you want until you are satisfied. In the meantime, you can call me Petrov. No one in the Federation Military knows me by that name, not even my girlfriend. The others will need new names as well."

"Well, Yoni or Petrov or Mother Goose, as you like. Any arrangements as to what happens to you must come from someone with higher authority than me before we can call you Comrade. You will be moved to an apartment with a guard. I believe that you might be more valuable as an Intelligence Resource officer than on the battlefield," Cheriolisky concluded.

"Nurse," Cheriolisky called.

"What now?" The head nurse replied after clearly having had enough interruptions for the day.

"We will be taking charge of this prisoner. I'll need enough bandages and supplies to treat him for a week," Cheriolisky suggested.

"In case you political bureaucrats have not noticed, there is a war on. If you are such a hotshot, get your own. What we have in this ward stays in this ward. He's progressing well. I'll give him another shot of antibiotics, and in three days, any doctor can take off the cast. He'll need physical therapy to get his muscle strength back. Sign off on this chart, and give me my bed back," she ordered while handing the Captain Yoni's file and a ball-point pen.

"How far is this place?" Yoni asked.

"Half a kilometer. If it weren't for your bags, could you walk that far?" Cheriolisky solicited.

"I hope so, but if I am to have a guard, give me a young man that I can train with. Whatever I am going to do, I need to be stronger than I am now," Petrov asked.

******

"No 304. This one is ours," Cecil Balinsky announced as he worked the four keys to unlock the heavy door.

Entering the space, Yoni saw that the apartment had two rooms with a sofa-bed in the first room, a tiny kitchen area with a gas stove and a small fridge in the other. A slim table with stools separated the kitchen from the double bed. A shower was in one corner and a toilet in another. Heat was provided by radiators. Over the cooking area, the cabinets were painted with bright sunflowers while the others were painted in geometric designs outlined in red, gold, and green.

A window fan provided air circulation to the cooking area, while a matching window at the foot of the bed gave both light and extra ventilation.

"We'll get a box of weekly rations, mostly canned goods, and if you have money, we can buy what bread we can get from the bakery, whatever the local farmers bring in on Friday, along with whatever meat, milk, and cheese we can find. I haven't been paid for weeks, so I don't have any money. We'll also need money for taxis and bribes, about 200 Grivna a day, I think," Cecil reported.

"I will need to get to a Sberbank to draw out some money, maybe 800,000 rubles, and get that money transferred to a new account with another bank under my new identity. Otherwise, the KBG will know exactly where I am. All I have now is maybe a thousand rubles." Yani explained.

"Your rubles will work here too. I can't do the bank transfer, but the finance people can through a Swiss bank that supports us. In the meantime, we must give you a new look, with a beard and long hair for your photo to go along with your new name, Petrov, and a new last name that won't be hit on Russian search engines. All of this is possible, but it will take some weeks. In the meantime, I am to help you get into shape," Cecil said as he pulled a stool from beneath the kitchen table and sat down.

Petrov's first outing on the cobblestoned streets was slow and halting as he had to carefully place the tip of his cane at the intersection of the smoothed cobblestones before he could take another step. As he passed others, several people touched their caps or gave a knowing nod of the head in recognition of the wounded veteran. At the cabstand, Cecil hailed a Volga, and others stood aside as he helped Petrov maneuver his cast into the vehicle.

Through his one eye, Petrov saw areas where Russian bombs had taken out rows of buildings, with some apartment buildings having their entire sides blown off, showing tattered remnants of thousands of former lives still hanging on their walls.

"The Russians hit us with something almost every day. Some of the women and children have gone to other countries, but others have remained to take the place of men who are fighting on the front," Cecil informed.

"The driver rolled down the window between the driver's seat and the passenger compartment and asked, "You young men, do you want to find some bar flies? I can find you anything that you want."

"No. Not yet. My friend's injuries will not let him have sex. We need to find a market where we can buy some food," Cecil explained.

"Most farmers come in on Friday, but a few bring their carts in whenever their crops are ready. It's just a matter of finding them. I can take you to the square. Someone probably set up there, but it is late. They sell out in a hurry. If we go further out, I know a farmer, and you can buy directly from him," the driver suggested.

During the next month, Petrov's transformation became more complete. His cast and face bandages were gone, and he and Cecil were doing longer runs through the parks, and Petrov was lifting a pair of dumbbells to help restore the arms. Sometimes they wrestled in the park, which usually drew a crowd who often bet on the winner. Cecil took all of the early matches, but as Petrov's strength returned, he dominated his smaller opponent. Although Cecil could still do some fancy footwork and throw him, he could no longer keep him down for the count.

"Petrov, you will have a visitor today from the American CIA. What you have told our people has checked out, and we have assured them that you might be a valuable asset. Do you want me to translate, or is your English good enough for you to talk to him by yourself?" Cecil asked.

"I will enjoy speaking English again. It has been some time. I would feel better if you hung around. There are some American accents that I have trouble with," Petrov assented.

The next day, Travis Spencer arrived dressed in a lightweight brown suit and open open-collared brown shirt with a US flag lapel pin. He was carrying a bulging leather briefcase. When he rang the apartment, he asked Cecil for help, and when they returned, he was carrying a large briefcase and Cecil was lugging a large aluminum case into the room.

"Mr. Petrov, I am Travis Spencer with the Central Intelligence Agency of the U.S. Government. I have been authorized to offer you work in the United States as an Arctic survival expert and operative. I would like to give you a polygraph test to confirm essential details of your story. If what you say contradicts your previous statements, I will examine you further on those points. Do you agree?"

"Do I have a choice?" Petrov questioned.

"Not really. Since you have said that you do not want to go into combat against your former comrades, you will be sent back to be hanged as a traitor and murderer. The Ukrainian State will not protect you," Travis flatly explained.

"Very well," Petrov assented.

"Try to relax as much as possible and speak plainly. If you do not understand a question, Cecil can help you, but he cannot speak for you. We will start after I count from ten," Travis counted down and began.

The early questions were softball questions about his name, place of birth, and his real and adopted parents. Things became more difficult when he was asked, "Do you have children?"

"I don't know, but I believe I may have a son by Nina, the wife of Mikhail Dulikan. We had sex with his permission, and she told me that I had given them a good, strong son to look after them in their old age. They believed it to be true, and she gave me a Yupik doll to keep me safe on my journey. For whatever spirits there are, I believe that I have some mission to preserve The Russian State as a free association of independent republics, not Putin's private empire. I am sorry for the long answer," Petrov concluded.

"So you may have a child among the Nanai?" Travis asked.

"Yes. I may. I don't know," Petrov answered.

"How is it that you came under the protection of the Tong leader Wei? I understand that he gave you a ring?" Travis continued.

"That is correct. When Mikhail and I were at his trading ship, one of his employees took the smallest piece, the tip, of my ivory tusk. I noticed that it was missing. Wei became very upset that one of his people had attempted to steal from his clients. That man was killed and thrown overboard, and his hands and heart were brought in on a silver plate and placed before a statue of Guan Yu.

"In recompense, Wei gave us both rings and safe passage to the Green Dragon Inn, where I met my twin brother, Yoni Rabinowitz, who was drunk in the bar. I took him to my room, and later met his father," Petrov said.

"Why didn't you kill him and take his papers? That would have been simpler," Travis stated.

"Physically, I could have. But there was no need. His paperwork allowed me to go to Ukraine, which I otherwise would have found very difficult to do. I was able to arrange through Wei that the real Yoni Rabinowitz go to New York to continue his rabbinical studies. He does not know that I am his twin, although I think that he somehow feels that we are. I do not know where he is," Petrov replied as a look of concern flashed across his face.

"We are going to have to put him under witness protection, too. If they look in New York, they will have him in an instant, and your cover will be blown. Both of you are going to have to disappear," Travis concluded.

"Witness protection? I do not know what that is," Petrov asked.

"That is a program where you both will be given new identities and put in a safe place somewhere in America to start new lives. The CIA will support you for two years, but after that, you will have to find a way to make your own living. You cannot contact anyone you know for 10 years. We may have to fake your brother's death to keep the KBG from looking for him. He will likewise be told that you are dead," Travis answered.

"It will all be a bunch of lies," Petrov concluded.

"That is correct. Now we will return to the questions," Travis continued.

"If you are under Wei's protection, will you sell him secret information if he asks for it?" Travis probed.

"No. I would not expect him to ask. If that was his intention, he could have turned me in to the Russians while I was still there and collected the reward, and kept the money he paid for the ivory. I will not knowingly betray the US. If he were to ask, I would return the ring with apologies."

"What is your trade?" was the question that started the next line of investigation.

"I worked with my Stepfather repairing anything that the villagers brought in, from clocks to tractor parts. I am a skilled machinist and blacksmith. If I can see something, I can make it or figure out some other way to make it work. My stepfather also built short-wave radios so we could listen to Voice of America and other programs in English as well as talk to others around the world. We never used the talk function because then the transmitter could have been traced back to us. I have one concealed in the bottom of the trunk that Moshi sent me. I don't know much about the more modern circuit-board stuff other than to swap them out, but I can build and maintain the old tube sets. I have also worked to repair most of the older Soviet weapons that the local troops would bring in. It was faster for us to do it than to send them to Moscow or Tula, which could take a year to be returned, as everything from the war in Ukraine had priority," Petrov explained.

"Have you ever received training as an actor?" Travis questioned.

"Only in school, like everyone else. We would do plays, usually based on religious or patriotic themes," Petrov replied.

"Other than your friend Sokolov, that you have told us about, have you ever been in contact with or trained by a KBG, FSV, or other Federation agent?" Travis probed.

"No. I have not," Petrov replied.

"You are quite sure on this point. You have never been in contact with another Federation agent?" Travis suggested.

"No. Never," Petrov affirmed.

"Congratulations. You have passed the polygraph test. As fantastic as your story is, every indication is that you believe that it is true. We plan to offer you a commission as a Captain in the Army to teach at military bases in Alaska. This will enable you to live and start a family in the U.S. How do you feel about that?" Travis asked.

"For me to take an officer's role would be a betrayal of my country and a disrespect to the rank. I am a corporal and content to remain as long as I have enough money to live on. This is about a duty that I owe to Russia and God, and not about money or power. I do not yet know what tasks God has in mind for me, to have spared me from capture and death, but that will be revealed in time. I was told that in a dream, and I believe it. Only by accomplishing this aim can I be absolved of the crimes that I have committed," Petrov confessed.

"And you believe your fate is controlled by God. Which one? Are you Pagan, Orthodox, Jewish, Christian, Buddhist, or something else?

"I do not know, but I sometimes feel his presence and reassurance when I am troubled. I want to make sure that the lives of men who have died to get me this far on my journey will not be wasted. That is the reality that I deal with. In my heart, I feel that I am a good, moral man who has been forced to murder three people and steal their money. This is my torment, and this is my strength. I want to go to church before I leave. I need to refresh my soul," Petrov pleaded.

"That can be arranged so long as you do not go to confession. Not even a priest can be trusted these days. I will arrange your transportation to the US on a military aircraft. You will be met when you arrive by another agent who will take you to the base where you will be assigned," Travis said.

******

Before they left, Cecil took Petrov to St. Nickolas Cathedral in the heart of the city. The front and back were covered in scaffolding while the windows blown out by the blast from a nearby missile that hit a Canadian mission across the street were being repaired. The ravages of World War II and a subsequent fire had stripped the cathedral of much of its original finery, but a new organ had been installed where free recitals by resident and visiting artists could be attended.

Arriving before the mass, Petrov was impressed by the vast open space in the main hall with its high Gothic loft partly illuminated by the morning light. In the smaller space below, candles illuminated a more intimate area. When the Priest said in his homily, "Forgive them, father, for they know not what they do," Petrov sank to his knees and wept unashamedly. Those in the church saw, but his scarred face and burned hands told them that another war vet had sought, and this time perhaps found, forgiveness.

After the service, a man dressed in slacks and a sweater came up and shook Petrov's hand, saying, "Thank you. Wear your scars proudly. You have earned them," and turned to leave, accompanied by two bodyguards.

"Do you know who that was? That was President Zelensky. The President," Cecil gushed.

"He looked just like anyone else," Petrov marveled.

"That's why people love him so," Cecil confirmed.

"This will be our last night. What would you like to do?" Cecil asked.

"I would like to eat in a restaurant and have a nice wine," Petrov replied.

"We can do that. If we eat at mid-afternoon, the restaurants by the river will not be so crowded or expensive," Cecil responded.

Cabbage with Spam, potatoes, a small whole fish on the side, rye bread, and sliced fresh tomatoes with farmer's cheese and the house red wine served for supper.

"That was good," Petrov observed. "I'm pleasantly stuffed. I hate that we are going to part company. You have been a good friend. You take care of yourself, and forgive me for putting you in danger."

"It's just part of the job. These are interesting times. They will take you to Poland tomorrow. That guy, Spencer, will take you to the airport and see that you get on the plane. You will be met when you arrive in the States. Look for a man with a sign with your name on it. He will see you through immigration and customs. I know we do it here, but don't try to bribe the agents. That will get you arrested over there."

CHAPTER 11
RETIREMENT

Commander Jack Reynolds looked distinguished in his crisp dress blues as he and Liz welcomed those attending his retirement party at the Army and Navy Club in Washington. Blessed with a slim athletic build, his deeply tanned face with a prominent scar on his left cheek marked him as a man who had taken some hard knocks in life and overcome them. Even at 64, his stature and steel-blue eyes commanded attention.

Liz was wearing a flowing aquamarine gown with matching jewelry that Jack had bought when he was a Naval attaché in Brazil. Although now separated after their son's death and Jack's coming out of the closet, the pair maintained cordial relationships as she pursued her interests in developing low-income housing in Baltimore.

While the grand elegance of the club, with its marble, wood-paneled walls, polished furniture, bronze statues of past members, along with framed cover photos of distinguished officers, was a bit much for Jack's present live-in partner, Bruce, Jack was in familiar territory as he chatted comfortably with the uniformed men and women in attendance. His past experiences coordinating joint efforts with the diplomatic corps had produced a variety of individuals who came to wish him well. He realized that this leave-taking was the final act of his military life, which had consumed his interests for nearly four decades.

Air Force General Randy Campbell approached the pair. "Jack, I am sorry to see you go. When you can break away, let's talk. I have a job for you that I think that you'll like." Taking a step towards the Commander's wife, he remarked, "Liz, I hope that you are doing well. Your son's death and Jack's coming out must have been a double-whammy of a shock."

"It was," she sobbed. "Jack and I hung on while Danny went from skin graft to treatment after treatment and was in agony for months. When the end finally came, I was glad that it was over. I wasn't supposed to be, but I was."

Jack nodded to General Campbell as he took Liz into his arms and whispered to his wife, "I'm sorry to put you through all that again. Do you want me to take you home?"

"This is the last time I will play, the 'Navy wife', Jack. I wish you well. I really do. I'm with someone, and he'll take me home. Please don't put me through this crap again. Do whatever it is that you are going to do, and leave me out of it. I'm done with it. I did love you, Jack. In a way, I guess I still do. But it's over, and it should be. Goodbye," Liz concluded as she turned and left.

"I'm sorry," Campbell apologized, "I didn't know that would happen."

"Randy, you were always more of a pragmatist than a sensitive soul," Jack responded. "Give me a few minutes with my guests, and I'll meet you in the library."

Entering the library, Jack found General Campbell with a book describing the Doolittle raid on Tokyo in 1942, when B-25 Mitchell bombers were launched from the U.S.S. Hornet aircraft carrier to signal to the Japanese that their island fortress was not impregnable.

"Maybe you don't have to cut yourself off from the service, Jack. We have something under development. Our new AI personnel program, AIMST, has identified you as the optimum person to lead this project. You scored 79 percent because of your proven management abilities in handling cross-branch relations, experiences as a pilot in both piston and jet aircraft, and diplomatic activities," Randy informed his old friend.

"How would this sort of thing work?" Jack inquired with interest.

"Now that you are officially out of the service, you will be employed as a civilian advisor at a much larger pay rate than you would have earned, even if you had made Admiral, which we both know was never going to happen with the Trump Administration. If you hadn't come out, you would have already been promoted," the General concluded.

"I know only too well," Jack responded. "Truth is I need the money. Danny's treatments took everything that Liz and I had. It was all in vain.

Septic shock after those burns took him in the end. Once it started, there was no way of stopping it. He went through all of that for nothing. I wanted to take him to Oregon for an assisted end-of-life, but Liz would not agree. That was what tore us apart."

"This project will take at least three years. Part of it will be to test weapons and concepts on existing airframes to aid in the design of a new bomber and train crews, as well as to suggest advanced penetration capabilities," the General informed. "This will allow you to build a nice nest egg. You will even be able to fly again, rather than being stuck behind a desk."

"Hell Yes! That is just the sort of thing I was looking for. I've had offers from industry, but this sounds better," Jack affirmed.

"Who will I be working with?" Jack inquired.

"Because the AIMST program is so efficient, I asked it to pick the best possible crew candidates for the aircraft who have the mechanical interests and skills to get the test aircraft into the air and do the mission. It came up with some surprising results," Campbell informed.

"Oh. Like what?" Jack inquired.

"I'll tell you about one. He is a White Russian whose family was exiled to Siberia by Stalin. He was about to be conscripted and chose to flee. For a year, he eluded being captured and lived with the villagers. He ultimately surfaced in Ukraine, where he was identified by the CIA as a possible asset and brought to the US. He wanted to join the Army and was offered a commission to teach Arctic survival skills, but he refused. He wanted to fight against what Putin was doing in Russia, but was so conflicted that he felt taking an officer's commission was somehow selling out. As an enlisted man, he said that he would 'Give everything I've got to help defeat Putin's aims,' but would not accept a command. That in his eyes would have made him a traitor. There is a price on his head, because of what he had to do to survive, and he can never go back," Campbell said.

"If a crew goes down in Russia, he would definitely be someone I would like to have around. Most of my experiences have been in the Tropics, not the Arctic." Jack hesitated as he continued, "My question is, can he be trusted?"

"We've checked out his story. He killed three Russians and contributed to the deaths of two more. We've also run him through various psychological tests. He is strongly motivated and would be loyal to any project that would help defeat Putin's objectives. In fact, he should be arriving at Dover AFB about now," the General concluded.

******

Petrov was exhausted after flying from Powitz Airfield in Poland to Ramstein Air Base in Germany and then across the Atlantic to Dover Joint Air Base in Delaware. On both trips, he sat on jump seats next to a window while the interior of the aircraft was filled with more seriously wounded patients on gurneys cared for by a series of nurses.

Sleep had been almost impossible due to the constant movement of the aircraft as the Polish crewed aircraft passed through storms over the Alps, and he was glad to be able to go to a holding room inside the terminal where the chairs were not moving. He had some coffee, sausage, bread, mustard, and chicken sandwiches while another C-130 with an American crew was being cleaned, fueled, and prepared for a return trip to the States. Out the window, he could see another set of patients being loaded aboard.

Once more on his way, he did not have to look far to see former combatants who were in far worse shape than he was. Some were amputees with bloody bandages on the stubs of their limbs, while others stared blankly at nothing.

"In a way, they are the lucky ones. Those who can't feel anything anymore," he thought.

His thoughts were interrupted by screams or shouted orders as some patients would have PTSD episodes that tormented them. He knew what that was like and hoped that it did not trigger a similar episode for him.

"Nurse, could you give me a sleeping pill and something to put over my eyes. I'm so very tired, but I can't sleep," he asked.

"Yes, I can," she said as she went to her cart and returned with two capsules, eye covers, and earplugs.

"These are going to put you out. If you think you need to go to the bathroom before you take them or pee, do it now. They are going to make you groggy and unsteady on your feet. If you get up, do not try to walk too fast," She advised.

Petrov used the urinal cup, and the nurse placed it into her waste bin. After taking the pills, he was back at the snowbound trapper's cabin, and three red streaks of the northern lights were darting down at him seeking vengeance. He cried out when he once again saw the face of the young trooper who had begged for his life before he ended it with a blast of shots from the SKS.

"What's wrong?" the nurse asked as she shook him back to the reality of the roaring aircraft.

"It's a man, a boy really, that I killed. I feel that his spirit is still with me. If I sleep, he'll come back. Can I have a vodka?" Petrov pleaded.

"I cannot give you alcohol on top of those pills. Here is some tomato juice, that is the best I can do," the nurse informed.

"Put some lemon juice in it, salt, and pickles," Petrov requested.

"Pickles? What kind of medicine is that?" The nurse asked.

"That always worked for my Stepfather. It does for me too," Petrov informed.

"There are some packets of relish on the food cart. I'll bring you two of those if you like," she assented.

"Thank you. That will help a lot," Petrov replied with a note of relief in his voice.

The concoction worked. Bouncing between sleep and alertness, Petrov kept his personal demons at bay during the rest of the trip.

******

Arriving at Dover in the reception hanger just off the runway, Petrov saw a man holding a sign with his name on it. Petrov waved, and the man came to him.

"I'm Clint Morrison, your minder. I'll get you through immigration and customs, and then we will go to a hotel for the night."

"I need sleep more than anything. Here is the paperwork that they gave me, and I have a trunk. The trunk has a false bottom with a radio in it. I need a chair. I can hardly stand after the drugs they gave me."

"We'll go through the diplomatic side. Do it all the time. None of your bags will be inspected. Relax Buddy, everything will be just fine," Clint assured the doubting Petrov.

After a perfunctory look at his paperwork and a scan of his face, the Diplomatic Inspector passed Clint and Petrov with a parting "Welcome to America."

Now feeling like a wet dishrag, Petrov collapsed in the wheelchair and was taken to a waiting car, where he was driven to a nearby hotel. Once in the room, Clint helped him out of his clothes and to a huge bed, into which he collapsed and finally slept, confident that he was safe in America.

******

Bruce was waiting for Jack when he returned to the apartment. He was wearing a caftan with a foral print and a pair of flip-flops as he leafed through the latest issue of Vanity Fair. Hearing the rattle of keys in the door, he opened it and welcomed Jack back home.

"How'd things go? I know you were not looking forward to this?" he asked.

"You didn't have to wait up. I'm all right," Jack responded.

"Well, I did, and that's that," Bruce answered. "I'm no psychologist, but I know Liz was there as well as a bunch of people who stabbed you in the back, so I wanted to be here for you and offer you a drink and an ear to bend if you needed it. You can't keep all this crap bottled up inside," Bruce admonished.

"You're right. Help me out of this stuff, and give me a shot of Dickel. I'm near falling-down tired, but too mentally messed up to sleep. Something may happen that will take me away - maybe for years," Jack informed his puzzled companion.

Bruce was silent as he helped Jack out of his uniform. He carefully hung up the coat with its lines of metal and put the trousers and other clothes in the laundry. Jack put on a heavy bathrobe and started on his drink before settling into a gold-trimmed wing-back chair facing the fireplace. Bruce came in and sat on a sofa opposite Jack before he asked, "What's up! Are they going to send you to prison?"

"No." Jack chuckled. "Nothing like that. This would be a three-year assignment on a project that would have me on military bases around the world as a civilian contractor. I need the money, but the rub is it's unlikely that you could accompany me."

"Why not?" Bruce demanded.

"For one thing, we're not married. Secondly, even if we were a group that I am likely to be associated with would not respect me as a project leader if we were openly living together. It is not supposed to be that way, but that is how it is."

"Double diddly damn," Bruce responded. "Does what we have mean nothing? I nursed Danny after he smoke-jumped into that fire in California and got burned. I lived with you and Liz as we watched him go through hell with all those grafts and treatments. Then I stayed and looked after you all until Liz found out we had something going on, and she left. You're the only thing like family that I have, and all of a sudden you're going to throw me out like an old dishrag?"

"I don't know for sure that this assignment is going to happen," Jack responded. "If it does, you can live here until you reorganize your life. You are a good nurse and could go anywhere. I'm sure that you can hook up with someone else."

"Maybe if I don't get AIDS or Monkey Pox or Hepatitis or Herpes or something else while I'm looking or working," Bruce interjected. "Do you have any idea what it is like to work doing hospice care where the results are that all of your patients die. You get attached to them. You come to love and try to care not only for your patient but for the other members of the family, and even their pets. When it's over, you leave, and most of the time you don't even get a thanks because everyone is so tied up with their own problems. I was really hoping for something better from you."

"Then why do you do it?" Jack asked.

"Maybe because I feel guilty because I was not able to do it for my parents," Bruce began. "Maybe it's because I can, and so many others won't or can't. But even I have limits. There are only so many cycles of death, death, and more death that a person can go through. Now do you understand?"

"The health risks are something that we all face. You're a nurse. You know that. You can find other work. I can't do anything about that. I can do something about this," Jack said as he opened a drawer and threw Bruce a box of condoms.

"You mean it?" Bruce asked.

"Yes, I do. Let's enjoy each other while we can," he said as he slipped out of his robe, undressed Bruce, embraced and walked him towards the bedroom.

CHAPTER 12

CULTURAL REVELATIONS

"Do you feel better now?" Clint asked as Petrov sat up in bed and looked around.

"Yes, I do. I'm sorry. I don't remember much about last night and have forgotten your name," Petrov replied.

"Buddy, you have been asleep for nearly 12 hours. We are in no rush, so I let you rest," Clint assured Petrov.

Petrov threw his covers off and tentatively put both feet on the floor. He then asked, "You called me Buddy before. What does that mean?"

"I suppose the closest I can think of is Comrade, but this is a less formal designation to call someone that you associate with, like a teammate or co-worker. It is meant to be a friendly form of address, particularly in the South," Clint explained.

As he stood unsteadily on his feet, he made a halting step towards the bathroom, but his knees felt like greased ball bearings. Clint caught him before he fell and supported him as he went to the bathroom and sat on the commode.

This reversal of roles, where he, rather than Yoni, was the dependent individual, was not lost on Petrov. With a parting "Call me if you need help," Clint left Petrov to complete his bodily tasks.

"I'm going to take a shower to help me get functional. Bring me some clothes and order some food. I'm starved," Petrov requested.

Freshly scrubbed with his hair washed and combed, Petrov found that a cart loaded with plates of scrambled eggs, steak, potatoes, grits, toast, and donuts, along with a pot of coffee, had been delivered.

Petrov quickly dug into the steak and potatoes, but hesitated when he came to the grits. "What is this porridge, and how do you eat it?"

"Those are grits. You put butter on them and maybe a little salt and pepper. A variation is cheese grits, where a sharp cheese is melted into it, and sometimes they are fried into a kind of pancake. In military mess halls, you will see them every day at breakfast, because so many soldiers are from the South," Clint explained.

"They don't taste like much," Petrov commented.

"No. They take on the taste of whatever is put on them, like butter or maybe ham gravy. To put beef gravy on them would be like a sacrilege. They are best when they are still warm," Clint offered as he took a bowl and doctored it up for himself.

"What are we going to do?" Petrov asked.

"The unit that you have been selected for is in training for a week. We are going to play tourists. I am to get you acquainted with your new country as we drive from here to Arizona. When you are ready, we will start in Washington and then head west. We can't see and do everything, but whatever you want to do, I'll try to arrange it. It's going to be just you and me all the way," Clint said as he finished up his bowl of grits.

******

When Petrov saw signs saying that they were approaching the Virginia state line, he said, "I'll get out my papers."

"That won't be necessary. You can travel anywhere in the country without having travel documents. Sometimes there will be license checks and we may stop and pay tolls, but except for military bases and restricted areas, you do not have to show any identification," Clint answered.

"Why in Russia, we had to show our documents and get permission to go anywhere. You could even be checked on the street without any reason at all. Often, you would have to pay a bribe to get out of it," Petrov stated with a questioning look on his face.

"That wasn't the case here until the Trump administration. Now immigration agents, ICE, and sometimes police and guardsmen may ask anyone for proof of citizenship and deport non-citizens who have overstayed their visas or committed crimes," Clint replied.

"I have heard of and read things from the Smithsonian Museum. I would like to visit the Air and Space Museum. I have always been interested in flying, but never had the opportunity to even be on an airplane until I came here," Petrov requested.

"That's easy. We'll do that this afternoon and then start west," Clint agreed.

Before leaving the SUV in the parking garage, Petrov asked, "I have never seen so many black people. The only ones we saw in Russia or Ukraine were students. Most Russians would not have anything to do with them. How are they regarded here? I know Obama was elected President. Is everything O.K. here now?" Petrov asked.

"The issues of slavery, forced integration of public schools, and incorporation of blacks into the U.S. armed forces are not yet fully resolved and may never be. About 20 percent of the enlisted ranks in the services are black, but only about 10 percent are officers. Prejudice against blacks is still common in the northern states where there are fewer of them, but it is becoming less common in the southern states where the population has dealt with this issue the longest. Interracial marriages are now common, as are mixed-race adoptions. These issues are improving, but problems still exist. This is our history, and it cannot be forgotten or erased. Never use the word 'nigger' or even 'Negro' as these are now considered insults unless used by blacks among themselves," Clint explained.

Stopping for gas at a Chevron fuel plaza on the interstate, Petrov watched as a man in a station wagon pulled up nearby and got out to fuel his vehicle while his wife and two children went inside. The man had a pistol on his hip, while those who were wearing military uniforms were unarmed.

Petrov got out of the vehicle and whispered in Clint's ear. "Is that man a Commissar that he can carry a pistol while the soldiers don't have any guns?"

"No. Although regulations do change from state to state and even in cities, generally an American citizen can buy as many guns as he likes, except that the fully automatic versions require special permits for collectors," Clint offered.

"You mean I could buy a gun? Guns? More than one?" Petrov questioned.

"Once you are on base, you can buy as many as you like at the commissary, and there will be ranges where you can shoot. We want our military members to be conversant with all types of firearms. You never know in combat when you might need to use an opponent's guns," Clint explained.

"I see they have pizza in the plaza. I have seen ads for American pizza and would like to try one. Can you get one?" Petrov asked.

"What kind would you like?" Clint responded.

"You mean there is more than one?" Petrov answered with a note of surprise.

"Many, many kinds. You'll have to come in and pick out what kind you want and what toppings you would like to have on it," Clint answered.

Back in the car, they pulled into a shaded area while Petrov extracted a slice of deep-dish pizza with tomato sauce, cheese, pepperoni, black olives, onions, and anchovies. Heading Clint's caution to let it cool somewhat before putting it into his mouth, Petrov watched the cheese drip from the sides back into the box and smelled the complex mix of aromas coming from his meal.

Taking a first tentative bite, and then a larger one, he proclaimed, "This is soo good. I would be fat too if I ate these all the time. I have never seen so many huge people in my life. In Russia, they would be in a circus."

"It's true. We Americans like our junk food and eat way too much of it, along with sugary drinks like this Coke you've got. Robert F. Kennedy, Jr, the Secretary of Health and Human Services, is trying to pass laws to eliminate inorganic dyes and food additives that he considers unhealthy. Eating this stuff is fine as an occasional treat, but this is an American trait that I don't suggest you adopt," Clint advised.

Petrov walked through the Air and Space Museum in a reverent silence as he saw on the floor and suspended from the ceiling ironic aircraft such as Wright's biplanes, the World War I German triplane, the assortment of World War II aircraft from all over the world, and relics from the moon landing. He marveled at videos of SpaceX's huge rockets and booster recovery systems, which included landing on barges at sea.

"It's common in Russia to belittle American accomplishments and highlight those early satellite and manned missions that really started the 'Space Race.' I think America won. Can the United States remain dominant?" Petrov asked.

"That's questionable. The Trump administration is cutting back on NASA and on research in general. China could surpass our accomplishments in the near future and seems willing to spend the money to do it," Clint postulated.

******

Halfway through the trip in Arkansas, Petrov told Clint, "After all this flying, sitting, and driving, I feel I need to do something physical. Some real work. Do you have any suggestions?"

"Do you like diamonds?" Clint questioned.

"Yes. We have them in Russia, but they were all state-controlled. It was forbidden to sell any that were found to anyone but state buyers. I did mine some gold, but never found a diamond," Petrov reported.

"There is a place, The Crater of Diamonds Park, about 150 miles away, where, for a small fee, you can dig for diamonds and keep whatever you find. They turn over the earth to expose fresh material. Most of what you see is garnets, but some nice diamonds are recovered every year. The largest was a little over seven carats, found by a French tourist after a rain. How does that sound to you?" Clint suggested.

"Excellent. I need to get outdoors and do something. Let's go. I'm excited about that. It would be like trapping. You never know what you might find next," Petrov assented.

At the park, they went through the orientation and rented a wheelbarrow, shovels, and screens. They were told they could dig, but the sidewalls had to be cone-shaped to prevent being trapped in a cave-in by the loose material falling from above.

Picking an area near one of the walls, Petrov started digging as fast as he could. While Petrov dug, Clint washed, screened, and inspected the spoil, but could not keep up with the piles of dirt Petrov was shoveling out of the hole. Ultimately, Petrov cleared an area below the plow level where the heavy clay indicated that they were in fresh material. After grubbing, digging, and prying out a wheelbarrow full of the gravelly clay, Clint refilled the hole while Petrov screened and washed the sticky clay from the other minerals.

"How are you doing?" Petrov asked as Clint rested for a moment by leaning on the shovel.

"I'm doing all right. I am glad I bought those work gloves. Are you finding anything?" Clint inquired.

"I'm finding garnets and green crystals of what they said was epidote and amphibole. Nothing that looks like one of their diamonds. When you're finished, come up and help me wash the rocks. We only have two hours before they close," Petrov suggested.

An hour later, Petrov put the last shovel of dirt into a gold pan and took it to the washing trough, where he massaged the clay from the gravel and started the panning process. The green plastic pan he was using felt good in his hands as he swirled the gravelly sand, picking out the larger pieces as he went. He thought he spotted a diamond, but had to look twice to make sure.

"Clint. Come. I think I've found something," he shouted across the water passage.

Clint came over and observed, "It doesn't look like any of the other minerals, and it is really heavy, the way it stays in the bottom of the pan. I think you have found yourself a diamond. You lucky bastard. Don't try to take it out. You might drop it."

Taking the pan with the stone to a nearby attendant, Petrov pointed it out. The attendant drained off the muddy water, placed the pan on an incline, and shone a light in the back of the pan. "Yep. You got one, all right. I'll take it out and write it up for you."

Using a set of tweezers, he carefully extracted the stone and placed it on a piece of filter paper to dry. He then examined it with his lens.

"This is a nice diamond crystal. It's clear. I don't see any obvious flaws. Its weight is about a quarter of a caret. It would cut to about half that weight. We would buy it for $150. A mineral collector would pay more if you want to sell it online. I'll put it in this bag and give you a certificate. This is the nicest stone I've seen today."

"I'll keep it. I think that it means good luck for me," Petrov decided.

******

At breakfast the next morning, Clint spread an Atlas on the table. This is where we are now. We are about halfway to Tucson. We'll go to Dallas and then head west. What would you like to see?" Clint inquired.

"A lot of the American films that I saw were westerns. I want to see some Cowboys and Indians," Petrov explained.

"Once we get beyond Dallas, we will be in oil and cow country. This time of year, almost every town will have a rodeo. There are many different Indian tribes and reservations. They have a lot of autonomy now. Some run casinos, and all have distinctive crafts. The Hopi are known for their dolls and pottery, the Navaho for their blankets and silver smithing, and the Apache and Comanche for their bead and feather work," Clint informed.

"I should not be surprised by this now that I think about it. The natives in different parts of Siberia were different too, although the Soviet system tried to make Russians out of them all," Petrov recalled.

"It was that way here too for nearly 200 years, but now the tribes are reclaiming their heritage, learning to speak their languages again, and understanding what their ancestors believed before European diseases killed millions. This was not as heroic as shown in the movies, but it gave us the world we live in today," Clint opined.

Drawing his finger across the map, Clint said, "What we can do is go to Santa Fe, where you can get a good sense of the Spanish influence on America, then go to the White Mountain Indian Reservation above The Rim in Arizona, and then drop down into the Sonoran Desert as we go to Tucson. That's where those big saguaro cacti are that you've probably seen in the Westerns," Clint suggested.

The next afternoon found them in Stamford, Texas. There was no doubt that they were in the right place because the City Hall was decorated in red-white-and-blue banners with a picture of a cowboy on a bucking horse announcing the Texas Cowboy Reunion. The parking lot was filled with trucks towing horse and livestock trailers.

"I want a big hat, but shouldn't it have a strap to keep it on your head in the wind?" Clint inquired of the salesman.

"Sure. You want a real hat, not one of these fancy decorated things. We've got some Stetsons over here that will do you fine. Mostly these are black, unless you want to go pink for tomorrow, which is our 'Dare to Wear Pink Day,'" the salesman offered.

"Black will be fine," Petrov suggested. "No decorations. Just a leather band and a strap so I can keep it on in this wind," Petrov requested.

"I see you've got tennis shoes. Do you want some cowboy boots and a matching belt?" the salesman asked, eager to ring up another couple of sales.

After receiving a questioning look from Petrov, Clint replied. "That's up to you. Whatever would make you feel comfortable."

"You should really get some more form-fitting jeans to show off what you've got. Get more women that way. You're a good-looking guy. Why hide it?" the salesman suggested.

Embarrassed, Petrov looked into one of the mirrors on the wall and shook his head. "That's not what I'm here for," he replied.

"Man, that's why we're here. Procreate or perish," the salesman asserted.

"No. No. Not me," Petrov responded. "I have some other work to do."

"Check us out, please. We don't want to miss the parade," Clint offered.

Petrov felt relieved that he had been removed from the conversation.

As the cowboys, cowgirls, and horses paraded in the arena, they were decked in their glitter, finery, and silver-studded horse tack. Petrov was impressed with the slim beauty of the women racers. He came to appreciate how apt the term "Rodeo Queen" was when applied to these women.

"Don't even think about it," Clint advised. "Those women think more about their horses than men. Their motto is 'use-um and lose-um.' The average guy doesn't have a chance."

With a head full of bucking horses, fancy roping, evil-looking steers, sharp-looking cowgirls, and a belly full of tacos, burritos, and fajitas, the next morning, they were on their way to the White Mountain Apache reservation in Arizona.

"What did you think of all that?" Clint asked.

"The food had a lot of tomatoes and peppers. Some of them were hot and some were not. I can see why you would want a cold drink with them. I liked that Coors beer, although it is a bit watery, compared with what I drank in Russia. I do have a question, though: do they put burros in burritos?" Petrov inquired.

"In villages in Mexico, you can often not quite tell what you might find in your burrito. It will be whatever seafood was caught or animals were slaughtered that day. In Tex-Mex cooking, the meat is usually beef. In Tucson, you will find a wide variety of Mexican-inspired dishes, as each region in Mexico has different dishes. Not like Taco Bell where the menu is always the same," Clint informed.

******

In Arizona, they overnighted at the Hon-Dah Resort and Casino with plans to visit the cultural center and Ft. Apache the next day. Clint purchased a $50 card and gave it to Petrov. "This is my limit on gambling money. You can use it in any of the slot machines. Some will pay off in coins, but others use cards," Clint explained.

Petrov ordered a Lone Star at the bar and watched the casino floor. Most of the machines were the same size, but there were four that were twice that size and visually promoted big pay-outs with $100 bets.

Watching an older lady take her empty coin bag off her lap and leave a machine, Petrov told Clint, "That's the one. It has not hit big in some time, and it may be ready now. I want to try that one."

Approaching the machine, Petrov ran his hand over the sides as if he were approaching a large dog and spoke to it, "Are you going to be good and pay off?" before settling down on the still-warm stool.

"Do you really think that's going to help?" Clint scoffed.

"Maybe not, but it helps me," Petrov responded.

Wagering $5.00 at the time, Petrov pulled the lever and waited. Six pulls in, he received a $2.00 payout.

"They like to tease you along with these machines," Clint volunteered. "They'll give you small wins, but most often the player will lose."

"I think it is getting ready. Two more $5.00 bets and then everything.

"Your money," Clint responded.

On the critical pull, the machine rolled up seven cherries, blue and red lights flashed on and off, and a buzzer sounded announcing his win. An attendant rushed up to quiet the machine, asking, "Do you want your $500 or to continue playing?"

"You stole my machine. That's my money," an older lady with a cane protested.

"Mam. The seat was empty, and this gentleman took it. It's his money. If you raise a disturbance, I'll have to call security to escort you out," the attendant responded.

"Lady. I was just holding your place. Have a seat. Let me help you. That money on the card is all yours," Petrov offered.

"Thank you, young man. You have a blessed day," the lady responded.

"That was a kind thing to do," Clint observed.

"She probably needed the money more than I do. I really couldn't do anything else," Petrov replied as they left the casino floor and went to their room.

Going through tribal lands, Petrov saw clusters of small houses located near small schools, trading posts, post offices, and less often, clinics.

"Typically, the oldest and youngest live in these villages. Most of the men have gone to work in cities throughout the US. Many of them are construction or maintenance workers of some sort," Clint observed.

At the Indian Heritage Center at Ft. Apache, Petrov admired the intricate bead and featherwork decorating some of the clothing. Passing a display of silver which included squash-blossom necklaces, bolo ties, hat bands, belts, rings, and bracelets, he paused.

"I recognize the turquoise, malachite, and azurite from Russia, but what is used for the red beads?" Petrov asked.

"That is red coral. It is found in the Gulf of Mexico, now called The Gulf of America. You want to be cautious about what you buy at tourist traps. Some of the stones may be reconstituted or even imitation. It's better to wait until we get to Tucson, and buy directly from a Navaho silversmith or 'old pawn' from a trading post. We'll be there tomorrow." Clint cautioned.

CHAPTER 13
GREAT LAKES TRAINING

"This is like a fashion show," Commander Jack Reynolds thought as he looked out over the auditorium at the Great Lakes Training Base. Men and women officers were dressed in the uniforms of the Army, Navy, Air Force, Marines, and Coast Guard.

All rose when Brigadier General O'Donnell. came to the podium. "Please be seated. Gentlemen and ladies. You have all been selected by AIMST for a special four-week evaluation to become members of a new Air Force wing of three test aircraft flying as single units against potential enemies. To fulfill this mission, all officers must be able to use celestial navigation. Following this training, crews will be assigned and sent to your duty station. Sergeant Rian will distribute your paperwork and assist you in moving into your quarters."

Jack Reynolds rose to speak.

"Commander Reynolds, your question?" O'Donnell asked.

"I have two. When will we know what this is all about, and when will our officers' families be allowed to join them?" Reynolds asked.

"After the initial evaluation, you will receive your base assignment, and the families will be able to join you there. Those who are not selected will return to their duty station," O'Donnell replied.

Lieutenant Sarah Mitchel rose, and O'Donnell acknowledged her with a wave.

"You mentioned crews. When will the enlisted ranks join us?" she asked.

"They'll join you at your duty station. Commanders of each aircraft will select their crews. Following the selection, you will work with your crews, readying the aircraft."

Captain Tom Anderson rose and was acknowledged.

"If we are to be evaluated, what criteria will be used?" Tom asked.

"Outside of the usual physical and psychological exams, being able to respond to unexpected situations is the most important quality we will be looking for. A basic knowledge of aircraft and engine mechanics will also be significant. Use your phones to call tonight. No further use of cell phones will be permitted. Sergeant Rian will collect them in the morning." O'Donnell concluded.

In an often-renovated enlisted men's barracks from World War II, Anderson, who was now dressed in shorts, socks, and a T-shirt, introduced himself to his bunkmates.

"It looks like they want us to know each other really well. I'm Tom Anderson, a fighter pilot. Started out with F-15s and built NASCAR-style racers."

First Lieutenant Chen Wei, who was still in full uniform, held up his hand to speak. "Sirs, ur Captain. I'm a navigator and high-speed combat specialist, Air Force Reserve."

Major Sam Collins, now wearing only his shorts, responded, "Relax, Wei. The Captain is correct about seeing a lot of each other. Go get your shower."

"It's just well, ur, I've never been around this much brass before and never in the same barracks," Wei explained.

As Wei undressed, Collins spoke to Anderson. "I'm a B-52 driver. In SAC and in the Middle East. Promoted, demoted, and called back. I can't say I'm too happy about that."

"Neither are all those married guys outside on their phones," Anderson responded.

Outside in the gathering darkness, Captain Albert Swain was talking to his wife, Grace, "I know I said that I would be there, but the Air Force had other ideas."

"Air Force? You are a Marine. They said that you could have leave when the baby came," Grace angrily responded.

"I know. Things change. This will be only four weeks," Swain pleaded.

"Well. Just be that way. You've always run out on me when I needed you," Grace replied as she slammed down the phone.

Swain shut his phone off and walked away. Passing Captain William Fleckley, he apologized, "Sorry. Wife stuff."

"Don't I know," Fleckley replied. "Divorced with kids."

******

The next morning, all the male officers were at the base hospital for their physicals. They were sitting on benches lining the hall, waiting to be called.

"I think the married guys had a tough time last night," Reynolds remarked.

"Sir. I think you are the senior officer among us. My wife and I are expecting a baby any time now. She's in Pensacola. Any chance of my going down?" Swain asked.

"What's your specialty?" Reynolds inquired.

"Besides being a jet jockey, I'm a metallurgist working on lightweight radiation shielding," Swain explained.

"I don't know any more about this than you do, but I suppose that's why you're here," Reynolds postulated.

"I've been using a sextant since I was in High School. If that is what we are here for, I can teach you. Being proficient is all about practice," Wei offered.

Dr. Gardner dressed in his medical whites, walked into the hall with a clipboard and called, "Commander Reynolds?"

"Here," Reynolds replied as he followed the doctor into one of the exam rooms.

"Good luck Sir," Swain offered.

"I'm generally in reasonable shape. I picked up malaria in Brazil, but that's under control, and I'm certified to fly."

"Malaria can be tough to get rid of. The parasite can hide in the liver. I want a biopsy," Gardner stated.

"I'd rather not. I just got over COVID, and I don't want to provoke a return," Reynolds explained.

"You are going to be in mainly an admin position, and maybe we can pass on that for now. I am going to give you some pills to take if you have any symptoms. If you become symptomatic, report immediately to whatever military hospital you are close to. This malaria stuff can damage any organ in the body, including the brain. Don't play around with it," Gardner warned.

******

The next morning, the officers were once again assembled in the auditorium for another address by General O'Donnell.

"Congratulations, gentlemen and lady, you have all passed your physicals, and your security clearances have been verified. The information I am about to give you is Secret and is to be treated accordingly. The only part that you may reveal is that you will be assigned to Davis-Monthan AFB for a period of three years. Your ranks will be converted to their Air Force equivalent at your existing pay rate, plus flight time and moving expenses.

Today, we will start working on a concept where a wing of nuclear-capable aircraft of three different types will operate independently. The largest crew will have 13-15 members, including four officers. Two groups will have three officers and two enlisted, and the remaining unit will have two officers. Those of you who are B-52 pilots go to a table and call for co-pilots, navigators, and a weapon specialist. Those of you who do not fall into these categories join Commander Reynolds at the front of the room," O'Donnell concluded.

At his table, Reynolds announced, "I need a co-pilot, two navigators-electronic officers, a flight engineer, and two weapons experts.

"I'd be happy to fly with you. Navigator," Mitchel offered.

"Lieutenant Mitchel, whatever our mission is, you are going to likely be in an all-male crew. Is that all right with you?"

"No difference than anywhere else. No problem," Mitchel affirmed.

"Glad to have you. Have a seat," Reynolds responded.

"I'm Bill Hogg. I've done a little B-52, but also rebuilt old fighters from World War II. There is only one aircraft that takes a crew that large. I want a crack at it."

"Captain Hogg, you may be correct. We are apparently going to be rebuilding something. Have a seat. I'll list you as co-pilot," Reynolds affirmed.

"Thompson, weapons officer."

"Captain Thompson, offensive or defensive?" Reynolds asked.

"Defensive. Electronics, guns, and rockets," Thompson replied.

"Do you know of someone who is particularly up on offensive weapons?" Reynolds asked.

"I got a buddy. Let me get him," Thompson offered and returned in a few minutes with a slim pale officer who looked like he might be a college professor.

"Commander, this is Major Slade. He knows more about U.S., Russian, and Chinese systems than anyone around," Thompson informed.

"Major Slade, glad to have you," Reynolds welcomed.

"Sir. I'm a fighter pilot. I don't know how I am supposed to fit into this group?" Anderson asked.

"Same here, Sir," Swain added.

"The General said that a new-concept aircraft would be built. You may be their pilots. Go ask him. In the meantime, you can work with my group. I'll put you both down as flight engineers," Anderson suggested.

Anderson and Swain approached General O'Donnell, who was set up at a table in a corner of the room.

"Sir, Swain and I are fighter jocks. Commander Reynolds said you might have something for us?" Anderson inquired.

"Yes. A new bomber is going to be built with passive defense mechanisms for this mission. You two are going to be our liaison and help design and develop tactics for it," O'Donnell responded.

"Wow! I've always wanted to be on the ground floor of designing a new jet. What do you think of that, Swain?" Anderson questioned.

"Me too, but I've got a problem," Swain added.

"It's my wife, Sir. Grace is in Florida, about to have a baby. We lost the last one. I could not be there then, and she really wants me with her now. Lieutenant Wei has offered to teach me celestial navigation when we are assigned. He's been doing it for more than 10 years."

"You need to give this mission your full attention. You can't if you are worried about that. If you can get your instructions from Wei, that can work. Get packed. I'll have orders cut. Anderson and Wei can fill you in on what you missed."

At another table, Major Collins sat with cards labeled co-pilot, navigator, and weapons specialist in front of empty chairs. Wei arrived and stood at the navigator's chair.

"May I?" Wei asked.

"Sure. Have a seat and tell me about yourself," Collins requested.

"I was a member of a sailing club in High School and later did saltwater sailing with my college sailing team. I was called 'Sextant' because I always had my instrument, tables, and charts. I am also a high-speed combat specialist with a limited amount of stick time, mostly in simulators. I passed my flight exams on prop and single-engine jets, but that's it thus far," Wei related.

"Sounds good to me. Have a seat."

Another officer approached the table and was acknowledged by Collins.

"I'm a pilot with training in electronics warfare and weapons. The name is Bossinak Brown. You can call me 'Boss' if you like."

"How did you come by that name?" Collins asked.

"Momma wanted at least one of her kids to be boss of something. So she gave me that name," Boss explained.

"What have you been doing?" Collins asked.

"I've been doing systems upgrades on B-52s and testing some of the classified stuff," Boss explained.

"You sound like just the person we need. Welcome aboard. Welcome to you all," Collins concluded.

CHAPTER 14

DAVIS-MONTHAN AFB

Nearly 50 officers and enlisted men were gathered in the briefing room at Davis-Monthan Air Force Base in Tucson. All stood as General O'Donnell entered and went to the podium.

"Please be seated. I would like to welcome you all to Davis-Monthan and the next phase of our operation. The aircraft that you will be working with will shortly be moved into their hangers. Those working with B-36 restoration gather at the rear, and the B-52 crews assemble at the front."

Commander Reynolds, Captain Thompson, Captain Hogg, Captain Slade, and Lieutenant Mitchel went to the rear of the room, as did five enlisted men. All were dressed in their different service uniforms as they had not received their Air Force uniforms from the tailors.

"Who has ever done anything with the B-36?" Reynolds asked.

Everyone looked at each other, and no one responded. After a period of silence, Captain Hogg spoke up. "I've read up on them, seen a couple of movies, like the one with Jimmy Stewart, but that's it."

"I didn't think that I would be so lucky as to find someone who had actually worked on one," Reynolds admitted.

Sergeant Maria Gonzalez rose and said, "I've worked on large piston engines, but nothing like the 28 cylinders the Wasp Major has. They were sons of bitches so far as I hear."

"The plane that we are going to be working on has not flown since 1955. Fortunately, the engines were made up to the 1970s. We will need to replace or rebuild all six of the prop engines. The four jet engines should be no problem," Reynolds replied.

"You don't just tear into something like that and hope for the best," Gonzalez responded.

"There are manuals and training films. Our first task is to find them. We are going to be librarians and scroungers. We need to recover those training materials, engines, and parts from wherever they might be."

"Sir, I'll be happy to work on the engines and help you find what we need, but if we are going to do anything in a hurry, I will need an officer with some clout," Gonzalez explained.

"I can help out there," Captain Thompson responded. "One thing that worries me is that a lot of information on that plane's engines was never computerized. The service logs may be around, but where? Finding them is going to take time and people."

"The logs were flown down with the aircraft. We'll have the staff here search for them. Some things might be in Alaska at Elmendorf or at Shemya, where it was last based," Reynolds informed.

"Sir. I'm just getting settled in with my wife and kids. I can help find the local stuff," Captain Slade volunteered.

"For the next three days, I want the computer and physical files searched. Thompson, see to that. Sergeant Gonzalez start looking for engines in the warehouses here. Mitchel call bases around the world to see if they have engines in storage. I am going to contact manufacturers. Say we are working on a special application for the Air Force Academy. Keep in mind that we are going to be flying in this museum piece. We've got to get it right," Reynolds admonished.

******

That evening, Commander Reynolds got to meet the last arriving member of his team in his office.

"Commander Reynolds, I am Clint Morrison with the CIA, and this is Petrov, whom you have heard about. We have just completed a drive from Delaware to give Petrov a feeling for his new country. Here is his file."

The three sat down while Reynolds leafed through the documents, taking notes as he went.

"Mr. Petrov, you have led an interesting life. You are about to be exposed to classified information that you will be sworn to never disclose. My question, and that of all the team members, is 'Can we trust you?'" Reynolds asked.

Clint was quick to interject, "Everything he has told me has been checked out in Ukraine and in Russia so far as we have been able to determine. The department feels that we can give him a Top Secret Clearance."

"You eluded capture by the Russian police for a year, and apparently could act well enough that the Russian army accepted you as a drafted rabbinical student. How do I know that you are not acting now?" Reynolds continued.

"My parents were exiled to Siberia, and I was raised there. I was to be conscripted and refused to help Putin conquer Ukraine. My father and three others died during my escape. I was kept alive by a Nanai family, befriended by a Chinese smuggler, aided by a Jewish family who was trying to get their son out of the country, went through army training, was deployed, surrendered to Ukrainian units, and recruited by your CIA. I will do anything to defeat Putin's aim of world domination. I took an oath to defend Mother Russia against all enemies, and I consider that my life's work. If I must die to accomplish this, I am ready. No. Commander Reynolds, I am not acting," Petrov asserted.

"The name you used to fool the Russian officers, Yoni Rabinowitz. What happened to him? Did you kill him?" Reynolds asked.

"I could have, but I did not. I helped his father contact a Chinese smuggler named Wei, who arranged to get him to the US. I don't know what happened to him," Petrov explained.

"You looked that much alike?" Reynolds questioned.

"With a shaved head and brown contact lenses, we did. The army was not too particular about who they sent to the front," Petrov related.

"What position did you hold?" Reynolds questioned,

"I was a Corporal and the leader of the heavy machine gun squad. Lieutenant Androv also designated me as Chief Whipper," Petrov replied.

"Whipper?" Reynolds responded.

"I was to administer punishment to those who listened to illegal broadcasts, dealt in contraband, or spoke against Putin and the war," Petrov explained.

"Did you administer such punishment?" Reynolds pressed.

"Only once. Two strikes on the back of a man who turned out to be the Political Officer FSV agent in our platoon. He was shot when we surrendered, but he survived," Petrov related.

"What was the maximum punishment?" Reynolds pressed.

"Androv made sure we all knew that it was to be one thousand lashes for desertion. Each platoon member would administer the punishment until all that was left were bloody bones," Petrov answered.

"This was authorized by higher authorities?" Reynolds asked with an air of disbelief.

"This platoon discipline was well known but ignored. Deaths were reported as training accidents," Petrov replied.

"Do you have anything to add?" Reynolds continued.

"I feel that I have been spared by whatever gods here may be to stop Putin from destroying my country and the world. That is my mission," Petrov affirmed.

"Mr. Morrison, your duties are discharged. You can leave now," Reynolds directed.

"Goodbye, Petrov. We had an interesting trip. I enjoyed it. Take care of him, Commander Reynolds. We may need him for something else," with these words and a handshake to both men, Clint left the room.

"I have a concern. You said that the Chinese smuggler's name was Wei? One of our officers has that name," Reynolds noted.

"Wei is a common name in eastern China. Does he wear a ring like this?" Petrov asked as he pulled a ring from his pocket with green, red, and gold enameled stripes.

"I don't know," Reynolds responded.

"He might be related to one of the most powerful criminal gangs in China with worldwide connections," Petrov explained.

"The FBI gave him a clean background check. If he is a Chinese sleeper agent or Tong member, they did not detect it," Reynolds replied.

"I hope that they are correct," Petrov responded.

"I am glad to have you as part of the team. Now it's time to get to work on those aircraft," Reynolds concluded.

******

The following morning, members of all four crews got a look at the first of the three aircraft they would be working on. A B-52 had been brought into the hanger and one of its engines was on a dolly. A buzzing sound was being emitted by the engine.

"Damn. This thing is full of bees. If our engines look like this, we are in trouble," Hogg remarked.

"Nothing to be excited about, folks. We know all the biologicals. We get snakes, rats, lizards, bees, wasps, weeds, and trees all the time," Sergeant Sunny Polk replied.

"Can that engine be saved?" Gonzalez asked.

"Sometimes. By the time the aircraft gets here, these engines are usually near the end of their service lives, and we swap them out. Started one once. The place smelled like burnt honey for months. What wax didn't get burned off set around any part that wasn't moving. Won't do that again."

"I had bees in Russia. Sergeant, if you have the equipment, I'll help you get them out," Petrov offered.

"Go to it, Corporal. We'll pull that engine outside so you can relocate them tonight," Polk said as he rubbed his hands together in memory of the times he had been stung.

In a quarter of another hanger pressboard walls were going up to make offices and work areas for the B-36 crew. Piles of manuals were accumulating on tables while members in cubicles were making telephone calls. Thompson left his cubicle and went into Reynold's office.

"Sir. We're in luck with the engine logs. It seems like the standard life was 1,000 to 1,200 hours. A problem is that the B-36 used a pusher prop and crankshaft, and all the other aircraft that had this engine had puller crankshafts. Even if the props are the same, we need those pusher crankshafts," Thompson reported.

"If we have to, can we use the more modern engines?" Reynolds asked.

"Not unless we change out the crankshafts and balance them on either side of the aircraft. The engine cooling system was also altered over time, and depending on the year it was made would have to be hooked up differently," Thompson explained.

"If the new engines develop more power, as I suspect they would, what about the differential shear forces on the wing?" Reynolds postulated.

"With those jet engines at the wingtips, those must be the strongest wings ever put on a large aircraft. If corrosion hasn't damaged them, the wings should be fine," Thompson affirmed.

"Anderson and Swain are here. Ask them to help you find things while they talk to their design people. The new Trumper Bomber is years away. I need answers now," Reynolds directed.

******

A week later, Commander Reynolds held a mixer at his quarters and had directed that the entire team attend.

"Over the past few days, we have gotten our feet wet with this project. Each of the four groups has challenges that now appear almost impossible. Be confident that we have the resources to get the three aircraft that we are working on flying again. Has everyone got their housing straightened out?" Reynolds inquired.

"I'm in a motel in Tucson. I can't find anything that I can afford, and there is nothing on base," Wei responded.

"Anyone else?" Reynolds continued.

"They are still trying to figure out when and where I will work with the Trumper design team in Ft. Worth. I expect that I will be flying back and forth," Anderson related.

"The house they have me in has four bedrooms. Wei, you can stay with me, as can you, Captain Anderson, when you are in town. Captain Swain, are you and your wife settled in?" Reynolds asked.

"Yes. We found a place. For those of you who don't know, we just had a baby, a boy, and he is doing fine. I've got cigars for those who want them," Swain offered.

"You and Wei have some catching up to do. You can come to my house to work with him at night. It's absolutely necessary that you learn celestial navigation, whether you fly with us or with Anderson. That's all the admin stuff. Enjoy yourself and get to know each other. This is going to be a long project, and all were specifically chosen because you have vital parts to play," Reynolds reminded the group.

Petrov approached Captain Hogg and asked, "Sir. Do you think that B-36 is going to get off the ground? I'm hearing that it was the only combat aircraft to have ten engines, or needed them," Petrov suggested.

"After looking at that engine with the bees, I think they might fly on their own," Hogg replied.

"I got about five pounds of bees and the queen, too. I have set out the new hive, and we'll soon have honey. Don't know about the B-36. They haven't been able to move it. Rotten tires, I hear," Petrov said.

"Frozen steering and breaks too. And then there are all those old hoses, electrical parts, wiring, operating cables, pressurization, and on and on. In the US, there is a saying, 'When pigs fly.' I think that may be true here," Hogg suggested.

"In Russia it is somewhat longer, 'When crayfish whistle on the mountain.' It means about the same, I think," Petrov agreed.

Hogg erupted with a loud laugh, which caused Lieutenant Mitchel and Sergeant Gonzalez to walk over.

"What's so funny?" Mitchel laughed.

"We were laughing about getting that B-36 flying," Hogg explained.

"If I have to pull those old crankshafts and swap them over to the new engines, that will take a week if I don't have to re-machine them," Gonzalez offered.

"Maybe we can find some new crankshafts, so you don't have to take them all down. That will give us plenty of spare parts," Petrov observed.

"We're going to be drowning in parts," Gonzalez suggested.

"I think that I had rather be drowning in drink right now," Hogg opined.

"Did I hear 'Drowning in drink.' That is the kind of outfit I want to join," Anderson offered as he walked up to the group, nursing a glass of beer.

"Come over. I'll drown you all right," Mitchel said as she looked at Anderson for the first time as an interesting man.

"Many have tried," Anderson replied.

"OK. You Hotshot. What have you got?" Mitchel questioned.

"I've seen The Elephant. I know what we are up against. We need better than anything that this B-36 ever had," Anderson answered.

"But first we gotta fly," Mitchel responded.

"Let's talk about flying," Anderson suggested as he gently took her hand and led her away to the cactus garden.

"It's not about flying, you want to talk about. Is it?" Mitchel asked.

"No. Let's go," Anderson suggested.

"Not so fast. Are you attached to anyone?" Mitchel pressed.

"No. You?" Anderson's counter questioned.

"No," Mitchel affirmed.

"Your place?" Anderson asked.

"We'll do supper somewhere. Tomorrow night," Mitchel suggested.

"I don't have a car," Anderson responded.

"No problem. I'll pick you up. Six o'clock. I know just the place," Mitchel affirmed.

CHAPTER 15

REBUILDING A B-36

After cutting the seals on the B-36's hatches, Reynolds and Hogg went inside the cabin, and Petrov and Polk stood at the Flight Engineer's and Navigator's positions behind them.

"I've lubed the steering cables and pulleys. Maybe they'll work long enough to get us to the hanger," Petrov informed. "They looked all right, just old. All the wiring I saw looked intact, but the insulation is cracking off."

Reynolds pulled back on the stick and attempted to pump the peddles. "There is movement, but it is really stiff. Stick and rudder to the right, then to the left," Reynolds suggested.

"I think we got something. Let's go outside and take a look. I've got to get a face mask. This dust is giving me fits," Hogg commented.

"Right on about the masks. We all need them. That desert dust has gone everywhere. We'll have to live with it until we can get it into the hanger. Let's see if we actually moved anything," Reynolds said.

"We did have rudder movement," Hogg remarked as he examined fresh scrape marks.

"There is something going on down there at the tail wheel. It looks like an old patch on the fuselage's skin. Take a look," Hogg added.

Petrov climbed under the tail section and returned with a piece of metal that crumbled in his hands, "I don't know what this is, but it has been under acid attack, probably from leaking batteries."

"That's an old patch. Looks like roofing tin. I was hoping it would be in better shape. We'll have to recover that section. Stainless steel shouldn't act like that," Reynolds observed.

"Fuck. I don't know about you Sir, but if we're going to fly in this thing, we've got to do better," Hogg admonished.

******

Gonzalez was going through piles of folders in the hanger when Major Thompson walked up with a printout in his hands. "Sergeant, I've found two engines in Ramstein. They are new but have the forward props. They'll be here in three days," he announced.

"That's good. I want to get started on something. We will still have to find some crankshafts or rebuild the ones we have," Gonzalez replied, looking up from the stacks of papers spread across four tables.

"How will we know they will work?" Thompson asked.

"We will just have to mike them out. Petrov said he can machine them to spec and make them fit whatever props we find. We'll run them all on a test stand before we put them into the only airframe we've got," she said before returning to her papers.

"I'll keep looking for crankshafts. They had some in Alaska at Elmendorf, but they got tossed after the Good Friday earthquake. There has to be some around somewhere," Thompson postulated.

Reynolds was walking out of his office when he was stopped by Swain.

"Sir. Can I have a moment?" Swain asked.

"I've got to be back at the strip in a bit, but we can talk," Reynolds answered.

"They are still trying to decide where Anderson and I am going. I'm working on my Doctorate in light-weight radiation shielding. I would like a little space to continue my research," Swain explained.

"At the moment, we have more space than anything else. Two issues. Is the radiation source safe? How much room do you need?" Reynolds asked.

"I'm testing small samples of foils and composites, a few inches square. The radiation source is lead shielded and would be no problem. A room about 15 by 20 feet with electrical outlets will work," Swain replied.

"We can manage that. Mark it out on the floor and explain to the contractors what you need. What have you found out?" Reynolds requested.

"The effectiveness of the foils depends on the grain structure of the metal, whether it is cast, rolled, or beaten flat. I'm trying to discover the best combination of scatter and absorbing foils to see if I can find some combination that is better than solid lead," Swain explained.

"That could be useful. Build your lab and keep me posted. If you need some special parts or fittings, Petrov has the reputation of being able to make anything from watches to cannon. We want to keep as much of this in-house as we can," Reynolds assented as he left for the strip.

******

By the time Reynolds returned to the B-36, it had a new set of tires, and Polk had a tow tug hooked up. Hogg was already in the co-pilot's seat when Reynolds sat down and buckled up.

"Come on, Baby. Move for us," Reynolds said as he gave Polk a thumbs-up to start towing the machine.

The B-36 shuttered, moved forward a few inches, and stopped. Polk got out of the dolly and inspected the tires to make sure they were rolling rather than dragging. Satisfied, he returned to the dolly and made a circular motion with his hands before continuing to pull the huge aircraft down the runway.

"We're doing it for real this time. Let's get you home," Reynolds admonished.

"She's doing it, sir. She's steering. Maybe there's hope for this old gal after all. I can't wait to get her in the air," Hogg commented with a grin spreading across his face.

Two hundred yards down the runway, a large clank is heard as something fell from the aircraft. Reynolds made a forward motion with this hand for Polk to continue pulling.

"Now that we've got her moving, I don't intend to stop," Reynolds told Hogg and Petrov.

On their arrival inside the hanger Reynolds, Hogg, and Petrov were warmly greeted by the other members of the team. Petrov walked out with a small ventilated box.

"Congratulations, Sir. Now we can really get started," Gonzalez acclaimed, clapping her hands in anticipation.

"Thank you, Sergeant. We lost an under-panel on the runway. Go get it and anything else that may have fallen out," Reynolds directed with a sigh of relief and satisfaction.

Hogg spotted the box with air holes that Petrov was carrying and remarked, "I see you found a stowaway."

"Yes, Sir. A horned lizard. I'll feed him and put him back in the desert," Petrov responded.

******

At the White Sands Firing Range in New Mexico, Major Thompson and Captain Slade stood behind a new laser weapon connected to a nuclear power source shielded by massive lead blocks.

"Target acquisition?" Thompson asked.

Slade looked at a screen which showed a balloon.

"Affirmative. Balloon. Thirty-five miles. 20,000 feet. Five miles per hour right lateral drift," Slade reported.

"Fire," Thompson ordered.

"Got it, Sir," Slade responded.

"Next target, fire when acquired," Thompson said as the two watched the contrail of a rocket streak across the desert's blue sky.

There was no need to confirm the hit as both could see the orange fireball from the impact, followed by the noise of the explosion, which sounded like distant thunder.

"That was impressive. No human could have been nearly so fast on the target," Slade observed.

"Our problem is how are we going to get six of these weapons in the retractable turrets, nose, and tail positions instead of the 20mm cannon?" Thompson asked.

"NASA did a good job on the power source. It's lighter than the one that was tested in the 50s. It's the shielding that's the problem. How is Swain doing with that?" Slade asked.

"Well enough to start mass producing it. He's cut the weight by 75 percent and the thickness by half," Thompson related.

******

Four months later, the once-empty hanger was now crowded with engines on frames in various states of disassembly. Magnesium frame sections were being welded while stainless steel sheets were being cut and formed to attach to the hull. Gonzalez and Hogg were adjusting the valves on the 28-cylinder Wasp Major engine. Their coveralls were heavily splotched with engine oil.

"How are you two doing under there?" Reynolds asked.

"Good progress sir. This is one of the new forward-prop engines. We just finished putting in the new crankshaft and should run her up this afternoon," Hogg replied as he emerged.

Gonzalez, who was further under the engine, came out and said, "You may need to know something about the crankshaft that I found."

"What?" Reynolds asked.

"I sort of borrowed it from the Pima Museum. I'll give them a used one back after I polish it up," Gonzalez confessed.

"I think that I would call that requisitional ingenuity," Reynolds said with a smile.

"The Air Force Academy also had two new ones in boxes. I convinced the prof that what he really needed were two used ones so his students could study alloys, wear patterns, and forging techniques from the '50s," Gonzalez added.

"No problem. Call me when you run it up," Reynolds requested.

Petrov had just finished tightening the bolts on the stand that he had welded together to hold the huge engines. For added stability, the test frame was attached to four hold-down bolts sunk through the concrete runway pad. To determine how smoothly the engine was running, he had installed sock absorbers and rubber pads. The expedient of a welded piece of pipe and a plumb bob was used to trace the arc of the vibration while its intensity was monitored on an oscilloscope. Fuel, temperature, and pressure gauges were also attached to capture as much information as possible about the engine's characteristics.

"We'll give it six revolutions to fuel and lube the system and then attempt to start it," Polk explains.

The prop started to turn, and Polk told Reynolds, "Push and release the start button. Something should start happening. Everyone step back, and let it do its thing," Polk asked.

After the crew withdrew behind a blast wall, Reynolds pushed the start button and watched through a thick glass window as the prop started to turn. The first cylinder fired, followed by others in rapid succession as a cloud of black smoke billowed from the exhaust. As the engine warmed up, this was followed by lessor amounts of white smoke and water vapor.

"She's running smoothly. There is no indication of vibration from the rear end. Everything else looks nominal," Hogg shouted to be heard over the engine noise.

"Full speed for five minutes," Reynolds ordered.

As Polk increased the fuel flow, the prop became a blur, and the engine noise increased.

"Sounds good, Sir. I've done my best to match the air flow that we would get while we are flying, but we really need to get these in the air before making final adjustments," Polk explains.

"Back her off and let her cool down. One down and five to go. Good job, everyone. I know everyone had their doubts, but we are getting there. We are going to get the newest jet engines. These are more fuel efficient, which means we may use them more often than just at takeoff, but it's these prop engines that are going to get us wherever we are going and back. I know you all had doubts, but Buzzard 1 is going to fly. Yes. It is going to fly," Reynolds assured.

******

Back at his quarters, Reynolds paced around, picked up the phone, and called Bruce.

"Bruce. This is Jack. The apartment lease expires next month, and you will need to move out."

"O. Do say. I'm already gone. I boxed your stuff and put it into a storage locker, and cleaned up everything. You should be getting your security deposit back. I'll need to give them an address," Bruce replied.

"I'm in Tucson. I'll e-mail the address to you. It will be a military post office. How are you?" Reynolds inquired.

"So you are finally getting around to asking. Well, I'm terrible. I'm doing hospice in this damn town in Alabama. I've got two grandparents who are in dementia, a husband dying of something terrible that they don't know quite what it is yet, a bipolar wife, a son who has run away, and a dog that hates everybody. That dog is the only one that has its head on straight. At least I know what I can expect from him."

"So you haven't found anyone yet," Reynolds asked.

"No. I have not, and I am not looking. It's you I love, and you are the person I want to be with. When I get out of this hell-hole, I'm going to find you. There is not a US military hospital in the world that is not short-staffed. I'm being called. Got to go before they send the dog after me. Love you. Goodbye," Bruce concluded.

CHAPTER 16
FIRST FLIGHTS

A reviewing stand was set up at Runway Number 1 at Davis-Monthan for the first public view of the rebuilt B-52s and the B-36. Seated in the stand were a mix of military men, wives, and civilian contractors who worked on the project. Ranking officers were in the first row, and General O'Donnell stood at a podium as he addressed the group.

"After years of work, a change in administration, and personal sacrifices by you all, three historic aircraft that played vital parts in the country's defense have been restored to once again help keep the peace," O'Donnell began.

The two B-52s and the B-36 were lined up on the runway with the B-36 noticeably behind the B-52s. Betty Buster was first in line with Collins as pilot and Wei as co-pilot.

"Wei, you ready for the show?" Collins asked.

"Yes, Sir." Wei enthusiastically replied. "I'm anxious to get her into the air. Hope nothing falls off."

"That's the signal. Power up," Collins ordered.

The crowd on the reviewing stand applauded as Betty Buster roared down the runway, fired an array of JATO bottles, and started her assent.

"We're up sir. Everything looking good," Wei reported.

"Up gear," Collins ordered.

"We're off to Alaska," Wei said with a note of boyish enthusiasm as if he was about to open a Christmas present.

Next in line was Louella La' Cruel, with Anderson piloting and Massauro as co-pilot. As they began their run, the aircraft pulled sharply to the right of the runway.

"What's wrong?" Massauro asked.

"She's drifting. Something is wrong with one of the engine pods. Can't control her. Once we clear the runway, shut her down, and get everybody out of the aircraft. We've got a full load of fuel, and this thing could go up like a bomb," Anderson ordered.

"Roger that," Massauro replied as he began the shut-down sequence.

"Tower. This is Major Anderson. Take off aborted. Engines shut down. No other problems. Need tow to hanger," he reported.

******

Reynolds and Hogg in Buzzard 1 observed and received a call from the tower.

"Understood. Wait until the runway is clear before proceeding," Reynolds replied.

"What happened?" Hogg questioned.

"Don't know. No smoke, so maybe not too bad. Keep your fingers crossed," Reynolds suggested.

"We've got all ten running and need to get them in the air," Hogg said.

"Shut the jets down and idle the props. You can tell the crew that we are going to be here for half an hour. Maybe longer," Reynolds ordered.

"I've cut everything back and turned off the jets. It's a shame. She really wanted to fly," Mitchel affirmed.

"Thank you, Lieutenant Mitchel. We do too," Reynolds agreed.

After what seemed like a very long time, the message came to take off.

"Finally," Hogg said with a sigh of relief that the tension had been broken. They had been on short flights before, but this time it was serious, and they had to put on a good show for their audience.

"Bring all the engines up," Reynolds ordered.

"Ready Sir," Mitchel confirmed.

"Ready," Hogg seconded.

Buzzard 1 started bucking like a horse being held back by its jockey.

"Full power. Fire JATO when at the stand," Reynolds directed.

As Buzzard 1 rolled down the runway, its huge wings extended almost to the reviewing stand when its internal pack of 33 JATO bottles fired. With a screech and jolt, the bird was in the air.

As the audience dispersed, General O'Donnell circulated in the crowd and stood among the enlisted men.

"Sergeant Gonzalez, you and the crew have done remarkable work getting these aircraft in the air. After you get the issue solved with that B-52, you can take a month off while the planes are being armed," O'Donnell offered.

"Well, Sir. Thank you, Sir. We. They have. Thank you from us all," Gonzalez stammered.

******

Inside Buzzard 1, preparations for their shakedown flight were underway.

"Setting avionics at Elmendorf Air Force Base. Lieutenant Mitchel, do you have what you need for dead-reckoning plotting?" Hogg asked.

"Air speed, course, heading, magnetic variation, and the wind info are coming in. We'll compare results every few hours," Mitchel confirmed as she plotted their course on a map.

"Sorry, Anderson didn't get off the ground. How are you two getting along?" Reynolds asked.

"Fine, Sir. We plan to get married when this is over," Mitchel replied.

"Just keep it professional. You can support each other psychologically and technically, as you are doing, but you can't fly together," Reynolds informed the Lieutenant.

"That's understood," Mitchel replied.

"Position check. Bozeman, Montana. Three hours," Hogg informed as Mitchel unpacked her sextant in preparation for her first star shot.

"Take it, Hogg, I want to look around," Reynolds said as he unbuckled and walked through the navigator-flight engineer positions, waist gunner position, through the slide tunnel past the second bomb bay back to the tail. His objective was to see that Buzzard 1 was responding as a single unit rather than a collection of components that might raddle apart. On his way, he examined wing access doors and looked out the ports to see the propellers. Satisfied, he stopped in the crew bunk area where Thompson and Petrov were sitting.

"How does she look, Sir?" Thompson asked.

"Everything I've seen looks and feels stable. Where are you going to put the reactor and your weapons?" Reynolds inquired.

"For the reactor, the logical place is here, low down between the roots of the wings in the space under the tunnel. Two of the lasers can go in the cupula top front, two in the cupula back bottom, and the other two in the front and back," Thompson answered.

"The problem is controlling these things. They are going to want to shoot everything out of the sky within 50 miles," Reynolds stated with his wrinkled brow suggesting the depth of the problem.

"We need rockets too, Sir. But none that give firing signatures from the aircraft. The concept is Delayed Drop Firing Rockets, DDFRs, that are dropped from the bird, but do not fire their engines until they are 200 feet above the ground. That way, the rockets would seem to come from a surface launcher or sub, and confuse the enemy," Thompson suggested.

"DDFRs? I like the concept. Work on it," Reynolds directed as he turned to Petrov. "How do things look from your point of view?"

"Electrically speaking, Polk, Gonzalez, and I have replaced the old wiring. I have looked at all the control cables that I can inspect, and those were fine. I'm more worried about those than anything else. This long flight, cold, and lack of oxygen should kill any remaining biologicals as Polk likes to call them. I think Buzzard 1 is ready to get something to fight with. A beak, teeth, claws, or whatever," Petrov offered.

******

Returning to White Sands, Thompson stood on the stage with a drawing of the B-36 projected on a screen. "Our tasks are to install a nuclear reactor in the B-36 and its laser weapons. We will also want to test the concept of dropping a missile to near ground level and have it activate and fire from about 200 feet."

Allen Osweago, an older American Indian dressed in a suit and tie, stood, "I think that I can help. We should be able to modify some things we have with ground sensors and firing mechanisms. They would need to be pre-targeted so they could home in on a radar signal from the ground or air. What distance?" Osweago asked.

"We can't carry everything. Say 50 miles against incoming aircraft and ground targets." Thompson replied.

Berny Snider, a 30-year-old man with a deep brown desert tan and dressed in a heavily stained welding apron, rose to speak.

"They don't call that thing, The Magnesium Monster, for nothing. It has more than 5,000 pounds of magnesium in it that we are going to have to cut and weld. I can TIG weld it, but if a fire starts, there is no putting it out. I'm going to need access for me, room to work, cooling, and people to take that thing apart," Snider informed.

"We'll remove some of the exterior skin panels so that you can work on it," Reynolds agreed.

******

In Pentagon conference room 67, the Secretary of War, Harry Hendricks, and high-ranking officers of the Army, Air Force, Navy, and Marines are in attendance to discuss general readiness.

Hendricks opened the meeting with the statement, "It seems like problems with Russia, China, Iran, and in the Middle East are pushing towards the use of nuclear weapons. We have enhanced B-52s with stand-off launch capabilities, low altitude high speed bombers, and supersonic stealth aircraft. This combination, plus ballistic missiles, would keep any potential enemy guessing on how we might attack. General Campbell, what is the status of The Buzzard Squadron?"

"The new Trumper aircraft is still in design. We have the B-36 and two B-52s testing new defensive laser weapons and rockets. I have asked Commander Reynolds, who heads the squadron, to bring us up to date," Campbell said as he passed the mic to Reynolds.

"All three aircraft are now flight-worthy; they have been fitted with anti-detection skin panels and with passive navigational and threat detection capabilities. When these aircraft are in the air, they will have no active electronics that an enemy might detect. The new laser weapons have been installed on each bird and have proven effective at ranges of up to 50 miles. We are also developing DDFRs for launching tactical warheads against ground and aerial targets," Reynolds informed.

"Commander Reynolds, what are DDFRs?" Admiral Jones asked.

"These Delayed Drop Firing Rockets do not start their engines until they are close to the ground, so counterfire would be directed at a non-existent enemy. We have some in production, but have not completed testing. Early results are favorable," Reynolds related.

"This must be at a cost of reducing bomb load and fuel, which would restrict payload and range," Hendricks pointedly observed.

"In the case of all-out nuclear war, striking one target would seem possible, two would be more problematic, and more would be unlikely," Reynolds said in a carefully measured response.

"I could see developing a small low-yield nuclear bomb as a deterrent and threatening with a follow-up attack with a more powerful bomb," Hendricks suggested.

"That's a policy decision, but once we expose ourselves, the chances of making it to a second target are seriously reduced. We also cannot remain over target while the diplomatic process is going on," Reynolds said, trying to appear that he was not trying to point out the obvious.

General, what's the most likely lead-up to a nuclear war?" Hendricks asked.

Campbell drummed his fingers on the table before he replied, "Russia could use a tactical nuclear device in Ukraine. We could respond by using something similar in nearby Russia. They might respond by using something larger on one of our Pacific islands. Then we would hit one of their military bases in the far east. They would strike Hawaii. We would hit something in interior Russia. They would take out Cleveland. At this stage, neither side would be willing to give concessions, and the exchange would continue to become more deadly and involve most northern hemisphere countries. The entire planet would be at risk."

Somewhere in this, the Buzzard Squadron would play mop-up?" Hendricks asked.

"Against whom and at what would be a political decision. Once launched, it would be difficult to send a recall as satellite communications would be disrupted," Reynolds warned.

CHAPTER 17

WEAPONS

"Gentlemen, I have received orders that we are to complete arming the squadron's aircraft and disperse for deployment. What is our status?" Reynolds asked.

"I have the DDFRs ready. In the B-36, I can fit eight in the rear bomb bay with the nuclear devices going in the forward bay. The B-52s can take three," Patric reported.

"Swain and I have been flying the B-52s enough that we feel we can do a combat mission. As we can't carry but two laser weapons, we are going to need some conventional rockets too," Anderson offered.

"I had the same thought. If those lasers fail, we would be completely open to attack. I'd also like some rockets," Collins affirmed.

"If things get hot, we would have to fight our way out," Reynolds agreed.

"I love the plane, but the old gal flies like a brick. I don't want to tear the wings off that thing. After all, she is older than I am," Anderson said, smiling at his comparison.

"The Regeneration Group at Davis has done an excellent job of getting Buzzard 1 ready, and while the old Buffs are not fighters, they will get the job done," Reynolds observed.

"Where are they going to station us?" Collins asked.

"The B-36 will be going to Alaska. Petrov has worked with all of you. He will be going with us as a translator and Arctic survival expert. He also has on-the-ground connections in case we go down. One of the B-52s will be going to Sicily and the other to Diego Garcia. Let me know if you have any preferences," Reynolds suggested.

"If it's all right with everyone, I would like to get back to Sicily. I've always enjoyed what little time I've spent there," Collins requested.

"No problem. They'll take good care of us at Diego Garcia," Anderson replied.

"Very well. We'll go back to Davis-Monthan and have a week to settle everything. In the event we are sent on a mission over enemy territory, your families will be relocated to Australia," Reynolds announced.

******

"Wei. Come here, I need you," Reynolds cried out from his bedroom.

"Sir. What's wrong?" Wei asked.

"Get me to the bathroom," Reynolds replied with a palatable sense of urgency.

Reynolds puked into the commode, then sat and discharged violently. Ashen-faced, he told Wei, "Medicine cabinet. Pepto Bismol. Pills."

Wei fumbled through the cabinet, retrieved the meds, and gave them to Reynolds, who washed the pills down with a slug of Pepto Bismol.

"Some cold water. There is a bottle in the fridge," Reynolds requested.

Returning, Wei opened the bottle and gave it to Reynolds, who took a slug and scrubbed his face with a washrag that he had dipped into the water.

"You look terrible. Should I call an ambulance?" Wei asked.

"No. I know how to handle this. Tell everyone I've got the flu and will be back in a couple of days. They can call me here if they need anything," Reynolds responded.

"Are you sure?" Wei inquired, not wanting to take the responsibility of having his commanding officer die on him because he did not take an obviously appropriate action.

"Yes. I am sure. Don't tell anyone about this. I'll need you to stay close until I get over it. This is nothing contagious," Reynolds assured.

"I. I understand. Until you get better," Wei responded.

A few days later, Corporal Shaun Hanahan was finishing serving their supper.

"Will there be anything else tonight?" Hanahan asked.

"No. You can clean up and go home. Just leave us with our coffee," Reynolds requested.

"I'm glad that you are better. It's been a bad couple of days," Wei observed.

"That's just the way this junk goes," Reynolds said as he enjoyed the robust taste of some of the coffee he had brought from Brazil.

"It looks like this will be our last night together," Wei stated. "Sir. Ur. I don't know how to put this. Over the past months, I have developed feelings…"

"I think I know what you are getting at. Do you realize what this could mean for both of us?"

"I do. I've tried to fight it, but I find myself. Anyway, will it matter? None of us is likely to live through this," Wei pleaded.

"Once in bed, it did not take long for their held-back passions to be expressed, and Reynolds lay back with Wei laying across his arms. "This is the only time that I really miss smoking or even think about it," as he stroked Wei's back.

"Wei moved so that they were face to face and replied, "I will remember this for as long as I live."

"I hope that is a very long time," Reynolds said as he drifted off to sleep.

"Wake up, young man. It's going to be a busy day," Reynolds said as he shook the naked Wei by the shoulder, and Wei rubbed his eyes and ran his hands across his face.

"Yes. Sir…I'm glad we did that. I don't know. I don't know what to say. I…" Wei spoke as he searched for the words that would not come.

"Don't. Just go do your duty as best you can. Maybe we can have something later. There's always hope."

******

"Lieutenant Mitchel, does the flight weather still look good for Shemya, Alaska?" Reynolds inquired.

"Yes. It does, and the engines look good too. I think we're off to a good start," Mitchel reported.

"Mr. Hogg, open the safe and bring me the orders," Reynolds asked before Hogg unbuckled and went to the safe with the key Reynolds gave him from around his neck.

"The envelope is sealed," Hogg reported.

"Sealed envelope confirmed. Open it and distribute the orders," Reynolds directed.

"Going dark. Send mission start signal," Reynolds ordered.

"Coded signal sent," Thompson reported.

"Captain Hogg, what is our destination?" Reynolds asked.

"Alaska. Shemya Island," Hogg reported.

"Course and speed?" Reynolds asked.

"North 53 degrees West. Flight time, six hours and forty-eight minutes," Thompson reported.

"Shut down jets. Power down one through four," Reynolds requested.

"Jets one through four are slowing down. Power down completed," Mitchel reported.

"Announcement to crew. You all know what a desperate situation this is. Your families are being relocated to Tasmania. We must focus on our mission. Our deployment will be to Alaska. Move around the aircraft and check for malfunctions," Reynolds announced.

In the crew sleeping area, Gonzalez made her own announcement: "You have all worked on the B-36. Station yourselves in different areas, and report anything strange. Put on your badges and watch your radiation sensors."

After sitting down at the forward port wing root, Airman Whitlock looked up from the novel he was reading when he heard a loud snap.

"Hell, what was that? Sergeant Gonzalez. Something's wrong back here," he shouted.

"Get a radiation suit, oxygen bottle, and a splice kit. I'll send someone to help and tell the Commander," Gonzalez said as she ran towards the cockpit.

******

"Feel that?" Reynolds asked Hogg who was in the co-pilot's seat.

"What?" Hogg asked.

"The aircraft shuddered. It wants to pull to the left. I can't control her. Mitchel gets Gonzalez on this. Now!" Reynolds barked.

"She wants to fly in circles," Hogg observed.

"It sounds like a broken cable. I'll go back to the tail and see which one is loose." Petrov offered.

"Do that, but don't pull anything. That break may be closer to this end, where all that work was done," Reynolds suggested.

"What's wrong?" Reynolds asked as soon as Gonzalez touched him on the shoulder.

"A control cable has failed. I'm sending in a man with a radiation suit and oxygen bottle to splice it," Gonzalez reported.

"I can correct our course a little with the jets. Let me know something. I don't want to ditch if I can help it," Reynolds stated as he gritted his teeth in resolve.

"Hogg, Mitchel, give me half thrust on jets one and two."

"That's like pulling a wagon sideways Sir," Hogg stated. He was now starting to worry.

******

Petrov helped Whitlock out of the floor access hatch passage and his radiation suit while Dr. Angus looked him over.

"It's under the tunnel on top of the reactor where they did all that welding. I am going to have to go in from the other side and push down on the shielding to get at it. I can't do it wearing all this junk," Whitlock declared.

"Keep your exposure time to a minimum. We'll get you some Arctic underwear. Don't want you freezing to death either. You'll have 15 minutes," Angus stated.

Whitlock twisted his body as he moved among jagged bits of metal as blood seeped from multiple cuts. He clamped one end with the cable splice and then felt a tug on his safety rope. As he emerged, Whitlock swayed on his feet as Dr. Angus examined him.

"Petrov, get those clothes off him and bag them. Take him back to the quarters and wash him down. Bag everything."

"I got one-half the splice done. The other one will need to be done from this side," Whitlock said as he puked into a bag Petrov was holding.

"Help me dress. I'll go next," Gonzalez said.

"Bates, the smallest individual in the group, took the suit and said, "I'll go Sergeant. I worked in that area. It's my job."

"Very well. Get dressed.

Ten minutes later, in the crew sleeping area, Bates was able to report, "I. I. finished it," before collapsing in his bunk with Petrov and Angus attending to their patients.

******

Reynolds felt a change in the controls and told Hogg, "I think that they must have done something back there. She's acting normally again. Don't need the jets."

"Yes, Sir. Shutting down jets one and two," Hogg affirmed.

"Got things fixed Sir. Have two crew down with radiation exposure. Doc Angus says he is treating their surface wounds and has given them anti-radiation pills. They will be out of action for at least two weeks," Gonzalez reported.

"We'll take them directly to Elmendorf. Check with Mitchel about the No. 4 piston engine. She said it was running hot," he ordered.

"Shall I break radio silence and call the tower?" Hogg inquired.

"Use the classified line. Tell them we are coming in with two radiation casualties and structural damage. We'll need a hanger, an ambulance, and a cleaning team when we arrive," Reynolds affirmed.

******

At the Old Alaska Roadhouse just off base, Reynolds enjoyed an Alaska-size sourdough pancake that filled the entire plate with a side of moose liver sausage. As he was eating, he found what he was looking for. A series of old phone booths with updated phones that took credit cards.

"Bruce. This is Jack. I wanted to talk to you. I'm going on a mission and might not come back," Reynolds attempted to explain.

"Well. O hot diddly damn, yo-ho-ho. The world's coming to an end, and you call me. Big boy what do you have to say for yourself at long last," Bruce taunted.

"I just wanted to know how you were," Reynolds asked.

"O, just wonderful. Marvelous. That family I was with. The grandfather finally died, the father that I was looking after died under suspicious circumstances. His hateful, bipolar wife was tried, and I testified in court against her. She's in jail. The son was put in foster care. He said that they were trying to make a slave out of him, so he ran away and joined the circus, and their dog got put in canine rehab. But that is not what you want to talk about. Is it? Now is it? Really," Bruce pushed.

"I wanted to tell you that I love you," Reynolds said, exposing what he had felt for years, but never before found the necessity to say."

"Whoop de do da. So you have finally admitted that to yourself. Well, I love you too. I think I know where you are. I'm coming up and we're going to get married whether you like it or not. So there," Bruce delivered his nonnegotiable terms.

"I can't tell you. How did you..." But Reynolds did not get to complete his sentence before he was cut off.

"I've got a brain too, you know. It wasn't difficult. Your glorious Air Force could not help but put out a Press Release of you and that ridiculous airplane and said you were the pilot. They showed a picture of you and a guy named Pavlov, I think. You are not going that long without it. Is he your latest squeeze?" Bruce demanded.

"No. The man's name is Petrov. He is a machinist and Arctic survival expert," Reynolds protested.

"I didn't think he was your type. You like um younger. Was there anybody? Anybody else?" Bruce pushed.

"Yes. Before we left. But I will probably never see him again. It was the last night before we left Tucson," Reynolds explained.

"I'm glad you told me. I would have found out, you know," Bruce retorted.

"About where you are. There are only three airstrips in Alaska that can handle the freight car you are flying. The largest base has a hospital near Anchorage, the other has a smaller hospital at Elmendorf, and the third is at Shemya Island, which has a clinic that is always short-staffed. I am at Elmendorf now, and I want to get married. Then I'll transfer out to the clinic at Shemya. If we are going to be crisped during a nuclear war, I want us to be crisped together," Bruce declared.

"I won't let you," Reynolds protested.

"You can't stop me. What would you give as a reason? That I was your former lover. You can't say that without exposing yourself. If you do that, your precious command that you think so much about is gone. It all started to be just about the money, but that was never it. Was it? You wanted power. Control. Now the shoe is on the other foot. Get used to it," Bruce advised.

"You're right. Let's end it together," Reynolds acceded.

CHAPTER 18
DEPLOYMENT

In Louella La Cruel's cabin, Anderson was in the pilot's seat, Captain Fleckley was co-pilot, and Major Doyle was weapons officer as Swain opened the orders.

"Where are we going?" Anderson asked.

"First to Australia. Then to Diego Garcia. Gas up on the way to Hawaii, then to Guam for weapons and more fuel. Then we'll go dark for the rest of the flight," Swain revealed.

"Damn. That is a long ass flight. What is our flight time?" Anderson queried.

"Depending on loading and refueling, 24 to 30 hours to Guam," Swain responded.

"Everyone is going to get plenty of stick time. Swain, catch some sleep if you can. You'll need it to fly and take some star shots tonight," Anderson directed.

"This ain't the Hilton, but I'll try," Swain answered.

"How are you and Mitchel getting along?" Swain asked.

"Under normal circumstances, we would be married and maybe even have a kid on the way, but now, who knows? She's on Buzzard 1, and I don't know where she is. Could be anywhere. What about your family?" Anderson inquired.

"They were told to pack a suitcase and fly out. Tasmania, I think. I hope they're all right," Swain said with a look of concern on his face.

"Going commercial air, they'll likely beat us there, if that is any comfort to you," Anderson replied with sympathy. He knew all right because he was worried too, but there was not much else to think about on this grueling flight.

"Captain. Two engines running hot. Recommend shutting down numbers 2 and 5," Massauro said with a sense of urgency in his voice.

"Crap. Those are the damn new ones. Shut them down. We're between nothing and nowhere. We'll push on to Guam," Anderson replied with a sense of resignation.

******

"To crew," Major Collins began, "Listen up. Betty Buster is going to pick up her ordinance in Europe. Then we are going to go hot to Sicily unless something happens before then."

"I'm using conventional nav, but can go dark anytime you want. I figure we'll need recognition aids until we get on the ground," Wei reported.

"Boss. How are our engines looking?" Collins asked.

"Thus far, those new engines seem to be doing O.K.," Boss reported.

"Wei, pay attention to the fuel. They are supposed to use less fuel and extend our range," Collins reminded his Navigator.

"Brezny, how does Betty feel to you?"

"She seems like she's trotting and wants to run. We can pick up more speed should we have to, but for now, let's let those engines run in before we push them," Brezny advised.

"Weapons system nominal. Can be activated anytime," Quinn reported.

"Keep an eye on them. If they go automatic on us, we can blast our way through the entire Southern Hemisphere, and start a World War by ourselves," Collins kidded, but there was an underlying note of doubt in his voice about that laser defensive system. He was somewhat reassured knowing that he had a load of rockets under Betty's wings.

After Brezny brought Collins his coffee, he sat on a jump seat so he could talk with Wei and Boss.

"If the worst happens, what are we humans going to do?" Wei asked his older companions.

"You remember that line from the movie Jurassic Park, 'Life will find a way.' Some stragglers may be left on earth, and those on the space station might hold out for a little longer," Brezny replied.

"I was being trained for the moon colony before they canceled it. I got bumped by a load of goats," Boss revealed.

"Goats? You say?" Wei questioned.

"Yes. Goats. They wanted meat, milk, and fiber. It seems that goats reproduce better up there than we do," the Boss informed.

"How?" Wei responded as this comment provoked his interest.

"Don't know. Never had a chance to try. That's a job for young guys like you," he said as he playfully jabbed Wei in the stomach.

"One can but try," Wei replied as laughter broke the tension that had been hanging over the ship like a dark shroud.

Boss looked at his engine monitor screen and saw a red bar appear in the window for no. 5 engine. "Captain. No. 5 is running hot. Suggest shut down."

"We'll keep the thrust balanced. Shut down 5 and 4. Wei, when speed stabilizes, recalculate course and fuel," Collens directed.

"Fire. Fire. In no. 4," Boss shouted.

"Hit fire extinguishers. Cut fuel to 4."

"Temperature dropping. Fire out," Boss called with a sigh of relief.

"Collins to crew. We have extinguished the fire. We'll make it to Guam just fine. A little slower, but we'll get there. Just keep an eye on those engines."

******

Conference room 67 in the Pentagon was reoccupied, with the attending officers facing the greatest challenge that they had ever seen.

"The Russians have deployed a nuclear device in Ukraine. We responded with a low-yield nuclear missile fired at a Russian assembly area. They will likely shoot something back at us," General Campbell reported.

"President Laurence has called Putin on The Hot Line, but he refused the call. We have no option but to conclude that a retaliatory strike is coming. Somewhere in Alaska has been suggested. Any other thoughts?" Secretary Hendricks asked.

SAC Commander General Houser rose to speak, "If we go to full alert status, everyone in the world will know and respond in kind. From there, it would take only a sneeze to plunge us into full-scale nuclear war. If we make a limited strike somewhere deep into Russia, that would demonstrate our capability and show our restraint. The Trumper bomber was supposed to give us that capability, but it never got out of design."

"If we do an ICBM from a sub or from land, it would be instantly detected, and Russia and maybe China would launch everything they have at us," Hendricks concluded.

"Three aircraft of the Buzzard Squadron have been deployed. Using stealth and deception, they can enter Russia, drop a bomb, and leave the Ruskies guessing where they came from. Then they may talk to us," Hauser offered.

"So we do our strike, lose maybe three aircraft, and prevent a nuclear war? Is that your proposal?" Hendricks said as he pressed for clarification.

"There are details to be worked out, but that is the general idea," Houser affirmed.

"As I recall, this squadron was supposed to be used after a nuclear exchange when the enemy's communication and defensive capabilities would have been mostly disabled. Not when the enemy is on high alert and fully capable. This sounds like a suicide mission," Hendricks responded.

"That is correct. But hitting them now will give us an early option that the Russians are not expecting," Houser replied, using a roll of his papers as a baton to emphasize his point.

"I'll present this option to The President. You'll need to talk to your crews. Everyone must volunteer. I know Laurence well enough to be sure that he is not going to send anyone on such a high-risk mission without them knowing what they are facing. Thank you, gentlemen," Laurence said as he stuffed some notes into his briefcase.

******

In the briefing room of Eareckson Air Station in Shemya, the crew of Buzzard 1 was assembled for a situation update given by Commander Reynolds. "There has been an exchange of tactical nuclear weapons in Ukraine and Russia. Our mission has changed. We are to enter Russian airspace from a northern approach and drop a nuclear bomb on a largely uninhabited area of central Siberia and escape. All the crew must be volunteers. Comments?"

"That's impossible. We'll never make it to the coast. Every radar station in Russia will be looking for us; their entire air force would be available, to say nothing of ground-based anti-aircraft, ships, and satellites," Hogg injected.

"Sir. I've been working on No. 4 piston. I've replaced the oil feed line and checked the valves. The cable failed because the welder nicked it with his torch. We haven't run the new jets enough to the point where they overheated like they did in the B-52s. I would want to fix that, but the ship is ready to go," Gonzalez reported.

"We'll have to dodge all the villages, go low under the radar, hide in clouds, and appear on their radar like a flock of geese. That radar reflecting coating we've got will help. I would think we would want to go 1,000 miles in," Mitchel reported.

"Anyone else?" Reynolds asked.

"Sir. Before I left Russia, Putin was showing off his reestablishment of the old Soviet air bases with new radar, missiles, and expanding airfields on the coast. They also have icebreakers with radar escorting their convoys. This is not the uninhabited Arctic desert that most people imagine," Petrov offered as he visualized a nuclear bomb blast sweeping through a village.

"I know about the bases on Wrangle and the New Siberian Islands. We have intel on those. They have also done a lot of work on the Temp

Airbase on the mainland." Reynolds related. "Petrov, you can draw a pass on this mission. I know there are people you care about in Siberia, but our target would be hundreds of miles further south," Reynolds explained.

Rising to make his point, Petrov tried to express his feelings as briefly as possible, "I am loyal and remain loyal to Russia. This includes preserving our constitution. That hundreds or thousands must die to save millions is something that history has taught us many times. It tears at my heart. It pulls at my soul, but this is the task that I believe I must do to help defeat Putin's aim of world domination. I'll do it."

"Returning to the mission," Hogg began. "If we have to fight our way in, that defeats our purpose. We have to try to sneak in somehow."

"I believe our best approach is to wait for the first winter storm and fly in with that. We'll try to imitate a big Russian transport on a route from the North Pole research base to the Vostochay Cosmodrome in Southern Siberia,"

"In looking at all of you," Doc. Angus started. "The physical and psychological stresses of this mission are becoming apparent. We've lost two crew to radiation. Some of you are struggling with moral issues. But, if successful, this mission could save millions of lives."

"Very well then. All able-bodied crew will go, and all are volunteers. Eat, sleep, rest, and stay nearby. There is not much left of Shemya after the last tsunami. Walk around a bit if you like. Don't pet or feed the foxes," Reynolds admonished.

******

Petrov and Gonzalez were walking along an old runway when out of the waste-high grass a blue fox emerged and followed the pair.

"You're hungry, aren't you?" Petrov said as he dug a tin of sardines out of his pocket and poured its contents on the runway. The fox quickly came up, sniffed the food, and immediately started eating and lapping up the oil from the can.

"You know you are not supposed to be doing that," Gonzalez admonished.

"What are they going to do? Throw me off the island? Send me to Siberia? They're doing that already. We don't have much to do while waiting for parts. What if we can teach this fox to carry a line in case we have another cable break? This way, we would not have to put a person next to that reactor," Petrov replied.

The next morning, he went back to the runway with his pockets bulging with cans of sardines, a roll of heavy fishing line, and 10 feet of ten-inch PVC pipe slung over his shoulder. He poured part of a can of sardines on the pavement and blew on a whistle. At first, the only movement was the tall grass being blown by the relentless wind. Then a twitching nose appeared and headed for her lunch.

"What we want to do is to teach her to respond to the whistle and carry this line through the pipe towards the smell of food on the other end. What are we going to name her?" Petrov asked.

"Let's call her Line Runner. It's all the same to her, I think, and it will explain his potential function to the rest of the crew," Gonzalez offered.

"So be it, Line Runner. You are going to get food. I am going to build you a place to live, and you are going to fly."

"Not so fast," Gonzalez said. "Commander Reynolds will have to agree."

"If it will keep some of his people out of danger, I think that he will," Petrov said as he scratched Line Runner's back, and the fox lay down in satisfaction to allow him to continue."

"Got to give her a bath. Don't want to give everybody flees," as he saw two small black dots move up his fingers.

"I don't think she'll like that?" Gonzalez questioned.

"Compared to being here, where it rains and storms all the time, I think she would like a warm, gentle bath. I know I would," Petrov said as he gently kissed Gonzalez on her lips.

CHAPTER 19

IN HARM'S WAY

Arriving in Sicily with Betty Buster, Collins, Brezny, Wei, Boss, and Quinn sat at a table receiving a briefing from Colonel Sundra, Sigonella's base commander. "While you were in flight, a low-yield nuclear weapon was fired into Ukraine, and we sent one back into Russia. We may be attacked at any moment."

"So this mess has already started. We had an engine fire. We need that engine replaced and all the others looked at," Collins reported.

"If we start pulling engines, you are not going anywhere for a week. We don't have parts for the new ones," Sundra explained.

"Then we'll take our ordinance and get out of here," Collins replied.

A siren blast echoed over the base as the telephone rang and was grabbed up by Sundra. Sundra listed and announced, "Missile fired at Guam. Intercepted. This is no drill. Launch all aircraft ASAP." Hanging up the receiver, he told the crew, "Gentlemen, get your ordinance and get out of here. Call for in-flight refueling. Good luck. I think we're all going to need it," he said as he rushed out the door.

As they ran on the tarmac towards Betty Buster, Collins shouted orders, "Quinn, get our package, and get it on board."

"It's on the way, sir. I see it," Quinn shouted back, and he ran to the jeep towing the bomb and waved his arms.

"Boss. See that tanker over there. See if you can arrange for them to fuel us," Collins barked.

******

Boss headed for the tanker on the other side of the runway and found a crew assembled at the plane.

"You a pilot? I'm the Flight Engineer, and we have the rest of the crew, but our pilot and co-pilot are stateside," Lieutenant John Yellowknife explained.

"You're co-pilot now. Let's get her up. I've got a bomber over there that needs fuel. Priority one," Boss replied.

"You ever done this before? It's a tricky business," Yellowknife responded.

"I have been on the receiving end many times, but never on the giving. But you have? Right?" Boss questioned with a note of concern in his voice, knowing that a single slip could result in both aircraft going down in a huge ball of flames.

"I have. I've had some cross-training. Between the two of us, I think we can do it. Once we get lined up, the automated systems will keep us hooked up while fueling. Then we disengage and go to our next one," Yellowknife explained.

"I've always enjoyed hooking up. Let's go do it," Boss affirmed.

One hundred miles out, headed towards the Atlantic, the tanker and Betty Buster rendezvoused.

"O.K., Captain, you are very close; we are about to go auto. When the green light flashes, I'll hit the auto-fuel-control switch, and that program will take over until we are done. Take your hands and feet off the controls. A firm pull on the stick will give it back to you, but for now, leave everything alone," Yellowknife advised.

"That's tough. I feel like I ought to be flying this thing," Boss explained.

"Trust the system," Yellowknife assured. "It's just like being on autopilot plus-plus. Believe me, it works."

Boss did as he was asked and watched on the screen as the nozzle entered Betty Buster's fuel port and locked. He was glad that Yellowknife was watching the fuel pumping rate and did not see him sweat under his helmet.

"Thanks, Boss. Needed that," Collins said as he thanked his crew member.

"Glad to help. I'll catch up with you. We've got some other thirsty birds to feed," Boss said as he signed off.

******

On Louella La Cruel's flight deck, Captain Anderson announced to his crew, "Gentlemen, the shit has started. The Russians launched a missile at Guam, which we shot down. The base is intact and remains our destination. Go dark now. We'll reactivate immediately before landing."

"We're 600 miles out. I'm seeing satellite static. It was apparently a high-altitude intercept. Recommend reducing power to 75 percent on all engines until we find out what's wrong," Fleckley asked.

"Damn. Any slower and we'll have to get out the paddles. Reduce power 75 percent," Anderson ordered.

"Power reduced. Speed 220 miles per hour. Altitude 40,000 feet. East winds 130 miles per hour," Massauro reported.

Landing on Guam, Louella was met by a fuel truck and a tow pulling a guided bomb on a trailer.

"What are they giving us?" It is a low-yield compact nuclear stealth bomb with internal guidance. It has a stand-off distance of 50 miles. Like our DDFRs," Doyle explained.

"Wonder where they got that idea?" Anderson postulated.

"No telling," Doyle responded with a chuckle.

"What do you suppose the brass is up to?" Anderson questioned.

"Don't know. We could be carrying something with a much bigger punch than this," Doyle postulated.

After they landed in Guam, Louella's crew was immediately briefed by General Turpin. "Thus far, the nuclear exchange has been between US forces supporting Ukraine and Russia. You are to remain ready in case China should become involved. Your secondary target would be Russia with penetration via India, Afghanistan, Turkestan, and Kazakhstan."

"I didn't know we had fly-over permissions from those countries. They don't particularly like us over there," Anderson questioned.

"It's a sometimes thing. The diplomats are working on it. Let's say they have to offer inducements," Turpin replied.

"Do you know if our families made it to Australia?" Fleckley asked.

"I don't have any specific information. Commercial traffic is still flying. You are to fuel and go to an airfield 200 miles south of Darwin. Maybe they can help you with your engine problem. Sorry, Gentlemen, but you need to be on your way. We might not be so lucky next time," Turpin suggested.

******

On an empty runway on Shemya Island, Reynolds and Gonzalez stood in a blustery wind watching Petrov attach a line to Line Runner's neck after putting his crate back in the jeep.

"The fox's instinct will have it go into the pipe and search there for food. Put some sardines at the end and flash a light to get his attention," Petrov asked Gonzalez as the fox sniffed around his feet and then looked into the pipe. "Come on. Your lunch is that way. That way," he instructed and pointed.

Road Runner sat, switched its tail, and scratched itself behind the shoulder. Hearing Gonzalez blow a whistle, the fox cocked his ears and looked down the pipe to see a moving light at the end. Squeezing down to fit, the fox darted into the pipe, trailing the fishing line behind it.

"See, Commander Reynolds, I can teach it to do things. It will have its own quarters and not cause any problems," Petrov affirmed.

"All right. Take him to the vet and give him whatever shots he needs. We'll take him on as a mascot. Hopefully, we'll have no more control-cable problem, but he can come if you and Gonzalez take care of it," Reynolds acquiesced with a smile.

******

In Louella La Cruel's cockpit, the view was all air and sea with a few fluffy clouds between them and the tops of the waves.

******

"Sir. This place they're sending us. It's Fenton Airfield, about 250 miles south of Darwin," Fleckley offered.

"Never heard of it," Anderson replied.

"Looked it up. It's a World War II base that the Aussies use for clandestine operations. They were warned we were coming. They put down some pierced steel planking to strengthen the runway so we would not bust through with a wheel," Swain informed.

"Where did they get that?" Anderson queried.

"Left over from the war. Those Aussies don't throw away anything. Once anything gets down here, they're going to use it. They are like my parents who didn't throw anything away," Swain remembered.

After they landed, Louella's crew was greeted by Australian Major Brockworth. "You are to stay overnight and depart tomorrow for Diego Garcia. A team with spare parts and a new engine is already on the way."

"I assume that our target assignment has been changed to Russia?" Anderson questioned.

"I don't know. I wish I could do more for you here, but Diego Garcia is much better equipped than we are. I've cooked up a Potjiekos that I learned to do in South Africa. It's got a meat base, then layers of vegetables topped with mushrooms, fruits, and nuts in a cast-iron pot cooked over a wood fire. And we have a few frosty Fosters to go along with it, along with some homemade French bread. How does that sound?" Brockworth offered.

"Excellent, that would be a well-balanced, nutritious meal. What we all need," Doyle interjected.

"It made me hungry just hearing you describe it. That meal, a shower, and a bed would be very welcome indeed. Thank you," Anderson replied.

"Not since I left Survival School have I heard of such a thing. It won't be at my mother's table, but I thank you for the memories," Fleckley mused.

"What are these meats? They're different. I recognize one as probably an alligator, and another as a rabbit, but the third I don't know," Anderson questioned.

"I wanted to give you Americans a taste of Australia. You've got salt-water crock, rabbit, and a bit of roo," he responded with a grin to their new Australian crew member, Captain George Hampton.

"All good protein, and all good for you. Eat up, men. Who knows when we will have a home-cooked meal again?" Doyle advised.

Remembering his mother's admonishment, "When there's food, eat. Don't talk," Fleckley chewed his food slowly to savor its down-under flavors.

"Were you notified if our families made it to Australia?" Swain asked.

"Our communications are spotty. I'll get on a secure line and have a message sent to you. When you get to Diego Garcia, you might be able to communicate directly," Brockworth offered.

"I feel like the red-headed stepchild that nobody wants," Hampton remarked.

"Well, you do have the hair for it. I can assure you that the Russians don't want you," Swain quickly answered with a grin.

******

When they approached the twin runways on the Atol of Diego Garcia, Anderson remarked, "There we are, boys. I'd like to vacation down there with a hot chick."

"Well, if you want to get away from it all, that is the place. There is nothing to do down there but work," Doyle commented.

"That's what we're here for. Maybe it's a simple fix for the engines," Anderson suggested.

"It might just be a line or hose of some sort. We will just have to see," Hampton said.

"Yes. I want to look at it myself," Anderson replied as they awaited directions to their hanger.

Within four hours, engine number 4 was on a test stand outside the hanger while another crew was unboxing and installing its replacement.

Later, Anderson climbed down from the test stand with a twisted piece of piping junction in his hands. "This is the problem. They 3-D printed this part, and one of the layers was too soft," Anderson announced.

"These are in everybody's engines," Missauto said.

Lieutenant Lee told the group, "We have a shop that can machine these parts, but it will take days to get them machined and swapped out. Or I can 3-D print the parts using one from the new engine as a pattern and get those out today."

"Will they last longer than the old ones?" Anderson inquired.

"At least as long. I'll choose different materials. We can get you out of here day after tomorrow," Lee concluded.

******

"I feel like a date who was stiffed. They sent us up and brought us back. I heard from Anderson. They've identified the problem with the engines and are sending us parts," Collins informed his crew after they returned to Sigonella.

"Can we get Boss back? He is better with those engines than I am," Quinn asked.

"I'm trying. He's flying that fuel-bag around. He should bring the crew back here," Collins replied.

While they were talking, Chief Mechanic Sterett approached and said, "Gentlemen, it is going to be three days for those parts to get here. We can machine the parts here, but that is going to take some time," Sterett offered.

"How long?" Collins asked.

"We have one set of old manual tools. It will take a day to set up and make the first sample, and another to install and test it. Then maybe two days to finish the others. Once we have the machines set up, we would want to make the entire run and a couple of spares," Sterett offered.

"We can fly on six engines if we have to," Brezny offered.

"If we have six good engines, we can do a mission. Make us six parts, and the other two if you can. I want to put them on and get out of here," Collins said.

While work on the engines was being done, Collins was in the situation room, pointing at a large map of Europe. "The question is, 'If we are going to strike Russia, how are we going to get there?'"

"We could go over the top of Norway, which would put us against a massive multi-layered defensive network or up from Ukraine, where they would be looking for us, but have fewer defenses," Brezny suggested.

"When we did our strike with the nuke, we must have weakened their defenses. I would suggest that we go through Ukraine before they can replace them," Wei offered.

"We'll plan to strike through Ukraine, fly northeast towards Siberia, and launch our weapon so it will fall on a less-populated area, but one that is significant enough to be noticed. That's our plan. Work it up," Collins ordered.

CHAPTER 20

FIRST STRIKE

Reynolds stood before a corkboard to which was pinned a large map of Siberia, while the wind and spitting rain that Shemya is noted for beat a steady drumroll on the roof.

"Problems have been reported with the new jet engines, which require replacing a part. We apparently haven't run ours long enough to see it. A shipment is coming from the U.K. tomorrow. Lieutenant Mitchel, what have you and Petrov been able to put together about a possible strategy?" Reynolds said as he motioned Mitchel up and handed her a pointer.

"We need to go in with a Spring storm so that we can hit the radar on Wrangel and the New Siberian Islands and disable the station at the Temp base on the mainland. That would take half of our DDFRs," Mitchel said.

"I can program them to hit the radars, but we'll need to be within 50 miles. I don't know how they will react if dropped in the middle of a blizzard," Swain replied with a worried look on his face.

"I'm sorry we didn't have enough of them to do adverse weather testing. We'll go as soon as the ship is ready and the weather cooperates. I think this is the first time in my life that I have ever wished for bad weather. I had rather be a fair-weather sailor, but that is not our lot this trip," Reynolds replied with a grin.

"I hope we do not do any sailing. We would not last long if we went into the water," Petrov interjected.

In the hanger four days later, Gonzalez reported to Reynolds, "Sir. We've been working night and day on Buzzard 1. We have replaced the plugs in the piston engines, adjusted the valves, installed the new parts on the jets, and done a complete frame and controls inspection. She is as ready to fly as she ever has been."

"Excellent Sergeant. It looks like we have a weather front coming out of the Arctic that we might be able to work with. We have a departure time of 0300 hours tomorrow," Reynolds informed as he looked at his own watch.

"I've got more on that storm," Mitchel said. "The storm will bring snow, which we can operate in. The danger is that icing can bring us down. All of our de-icing systems on that new skin have got to work, or we are going to be in trouble."

"I've run simulations on our laser weapons. All six are hot. The reactor is stable and supplying ample power even if some is diverted for de-icing. I've run some additional heating wires to the flaps and rudders. They are live, but this will be their first flight test. I think that's all I've got," Thompson concluded.

"Russian radio stations have issued red-flag storm warnings. They say this is going to bring accumulations of a meter or more within 12 hours, and continue until it exits on China's southeast coast. All civilian flights have been grounded and ships have been sent to ports," Petrov related.

"The men with radiation poisoning are doing well at Elmendorf. Potential problems are infectious diseases, radiation, and trauma. Everyone has been healthy ever since you recovered from your flu. You will have pills and fluids for radiation. Do you think you will have any wounded crew?" Angus asked.

"Don't know. It depends on whether we have to fight our way out." Reynolds replied.

"If you're asking. I'll go. No telling what might happen or where you might wind up," Angus offered.

"Thanks, Doc. You have been with us all the way. I will be glad to have you on board. Petrov. You have been a great help, and we may need your language abilities. This will be a nuclear strike on your homeland. While we will attempt to limit casualties, hundreds of people who have lived very hard lives, clawing an existence out of this country, will die. Do you want to take a pass on this mission?" Reynolds asked.

"'Hand in hand, we conquer', is a socialist slogan that I was taught. In this case, I believe it. Fate or God has brought us together, and I feel that we have something to accomplish. I will fly with you. Whatever fate decrees for us, we will have it together," Petrov offered.

As Petrov spoke in the theater of his mind, he saw a village with wooden houses and muddy streets surrounded by forests sitting on a river filled with floating ice. Men, women, and children dressed in leather and furs were going to the boats to help bring in the day's fish.

"I've seen and suffered under the Soviet system. I saw what the present government was doing in Ukraine. If dropping one bomb can end this slaughter and pillage, I'm in. God help us all," he concluded as he crossed himself.

"I'll want you to work with Mitchel to monitor communications," Reynolds directed.

Launching in the middle of a driving rainstorm that threatened to turn into snow, Reynolds spoke to his crew, "Mitchel, collect everyone's cell phones and turn them off. We are now dark. You have your orders. If you have any questions, come and ask me. Reynolds out."

"Sir. Everything looks and feels all right. I've locked us in on Russia's North Pole Station. When we get on line, we'll turn south so it will look like we're flying from there," Hogg reported.

"We have five hours before we launch our first missiles. Find us the best air you can. No one else is going to be flying in this mess," Reynolds observed.

******

Gonzalez, Petrov, and Doc Angus were sitting in the crew area with Line Runner sleeping in its box with its tail covering its face.

"I wish I could sleep like that. It's going to be hours before anything starts happening," Petrov commented.

"I know you two have gotten close. Do you want me to leave you alone? I need to check on the rest of the crew up front. I'll see you in an hour," Angus said as he departed.

"Thank you, Doctor Angus," Petrov said as he took both of Gonzalez's hands and brought them to his lips.

******

In the radar room on Wrangle Island, Corporal Kolesnikov sleepily looked at his radar screen while the wind howled outside, driving snow against the building. An irregular blip appeared on the screen, disappeared, and returned.

"Starshina, I have a signal," Kolesnikov reported.

Starshina Olenxsivosky looked at the screen and thumped it, but the signal persisted.

"That looks like something coming from the North Pole Station. I can't imagine them flying in this weather unless it's an emergency," Olenxsivosky said with a look of concern.

"Should I sound the alarm?" Kolesnikov asked.

"It must be a flock of birds or something. I'll not wake everyone up this time of morning, or they will find an even worse place to send me," Olenxsivosky responded.

"Yes. They could send us to the North Pole. Wait! There is something else. Coming faster," Kolesnikov exclaimed.

Olenxsivosky removed a key from his belt to unlock a clear plastic box containing a large red push button, when a blinding white flash enveloped the room, sweeping it and its contents across the now flaming ground where the tower once stood.

******

At the barracks of the Temp Air Base, Major Ranckoff ran down the hall and stopped to pound on a door, "Yargovic, get your group into the air. We have been attacked. Execute operation Starburst."

Flight leader Major Yargovic was unaccustomed to being rousted out of bed in the middle of the night, and when he opened the door, Ranckoff repeated his measure even more urgently than before.

"What? How?" Yargovic asked.

"Our radar and tower have been destroyed. We don't know how. Launch your flight group and do a perimeter search with your aircraft's radars," Ranckoff ordered.

******

Buzzard 1 buffeted in flight with the noise of the wind increasing and creaking sounds coming from the wings and frame as the old aircraft fought to maneuver in typhoon-force winds. Reynolds's arms jerked violently as he attempted to keep his compass heading.

"You got it, Sir? Do you want me to take over?" Hogg asked as Reynolds turned, and Hogg saw beads of sweat streaming down his bedsheet-white face.

"Take it," Reynolds mouthed as he nodded his head in assent.

"Swain, Mitchel, Angus, help the Captain. Get him back to the crew compartment. Then come back and help me fly this thing. She's almost uncontrollable," Hogg shouted.

Lying on a bunk with Angus and Mitchel standing over him, Reynolds pulled a bottle of pills from his flight jacket and gave it to Angus, who glanced at the label. "Malaria. Why didn't you tell me? You know this stuff can kill you?"

Reynolds opened and shut his eyes in assent and pointed to his mouth.

Mitchel got the commander a cup of water, and Angus held Reynolds' head as he took the pill.

"What should I tell Hogg?" Mitchel asked.

"Tell him that the stress has brought on an attack of malaria. He will go through a period of very high fever and delirium. I can keep him more comfortable, but it will take time for him to recover, if he does. Tell Hogg that he is in command," Angus directed.

******

Leaving Angus with the stricken commander, Mitchel went back to the cabin where Swain and Hogg had exchanged positions.

"How's he doing?" Hogg asked.

"Not good. Doc says that he is in delirium and will be out of it for some time," Mitchel said as she relayed the doctor's message.

"We're too far in to turn back now. We will complete the mission. Agreed?" Hogg asked.

"We've got incoming aircraft. Should I fire the laser?" Thompson shouted.

"Yes. Shoot them," Hogg affirmed.

******

Instruments crackled in the cockpit of Yargovic's Mig-31. As the instruments started smoking, he fired a rocket. "Eject, Eject, he shouted back to Yuri, his navigator, and they ejected in time to see the burning aircraft explode below them. As their parachutes opened, bits of debris fell around them, threatening to burn holes in their parashoots. As one of the parachutes started to catch fire, they watched the remains of their Mig crash into the snow-covered mountain beneath them.

"Rocket, In-coming," Slade warned.

"Got it," Thompson replied as he fired the laser, and everyone in the aircraft felt the impact of the nearby explosion, which peppered the tail section of Buzzard 1 with shrapnel.

As the sounds of metal piercing metal reverberated through the crew compartment of Buzzard 1, Gonzalez shouted, "We're hit. Everyone all right?"

"I think so," Petrov replied. "We'll need to seal any leaks in the pressurized parts of the plane. I think all the damage is back here."

In the cockpit, Hogg asked, "That was close. Weapons check everything. Anything else?"

"We're being scanned by something along the coast. Maybe a ship," Slade replied.

"Use another of our DDFRs. Take them out," Hogg ordered.

"Yes, sir. It's on its way. Two minutes to target," Thompson responded.

******

On board the Amur, claxons rang as the crew was called to battle stations. The DDFR from Buzzard 1 struck amidships, which caused the vessel to break up and sink as the crew scrambled over the side to escape.

******

"Got it Sir," Thompson reported.

"I am going to go around it. I don't want them to hear us go over," Hogg informed.

"Damn. Something is wrong with the controls. She wants to fly in circles again," Swain reported with the not-this-again sentiment being palatable in his voice.

"Get Gonzalez and Petrov on this. It's probably another cable," Hogg ordered.

Mitchel made her way to the crew area, where she found Petrov trying to coax Line Runner through a hole to take a cord back to the tail while Angus stood over Reynold's bunk.

"They're burning. All burning. Women. Children. I'm sorry. Sorry. Sorry," Reynolds blathered.

"He has temperature-related delirium. He's in a nightmare in tropical hell. He will just have to work through it," Angus said with a sigh of resignation.

"We need to know our final destination. Will he be lucid enough to tell us?"

"I can ask him, but whatever answer he gives may or may not be correct," Angus offered.

"Tell Captain Hogg that we are working on the cables. Had two broken. We'll have them fixed in about 20 minutes. Maybe shorter," Petrov assured Lieutenant Mitchel.

******

At the Yakutsk Airport tower, four hundred kilometers to the south of Buzzard 1, the alarm bell rang, which brought men into the room who took their positions as Airfield Commander Georgy Karamazov announced over the speakers, "The motherland has been attacked. Our northern bases have been hit. We must do what we can to provide information on any possible intruders and support any aircraft that may land here."

Operator Technician Third Class Sminov looked at a local screen and activated a regional display board, which showed all of Siberia.

"Comrades. The storm has kept nearly everything down except for this cluster of fast-moving aircraft out of our Temp airbase," Sminov relates.

Karamazov walked up to the large screen and closely examined a blurred signal tracking irregularly towards the south. "What is this? This signal does not have a tracking code," he questioned.

"I have been watching it. It is flying in circles. It might be birds," Sminov puzzled.

"I don't like the look of it. Keep an eye on it," Karamazov directed.

******

In Buzzard 1's cockpit, "I am going to keep her low in the clouds," Hogg plotted

"We've got mountains coming up. Keep her above 12,000 feet, or we could find one in this soup," Slade urged his commander.

Gonzalez rushed in from the back, "Sir. We've got the cables fixed," she reported as she caught her breath.

"I've got to make a navigation fix. We can go up so I can get a fix on the horizon, make my shots, and come back down," Mitchel stated as she started to assemble her equipment.

"Make it fast. They might not know what we are, but they are sure to be looking for us," Hogg agreed as he pulled on the stick, and Buzzard 1 rose towards the sun.

"More jets Sir," Thompson reported.

"Captain, I have us located. There is a canyon below us. If we drop into it, we can play opossum," Mitchel offered.

"Very well, guide me in. Cut power by 50 percent. Either they will loose us or overshoot us. Either way, I want to burn up their fuel. Turn 150 degrees. Hold course 20 minutes. Cut fuel by 20 percent. If they slow to match our airspeed, they will stall out," Hogg ordered as he returned to seek safety in the blizzard.

******

This chase was monitored at Yakutsk. "Two of our jets are near that strange signal. They should pick it up," Sminov reported.

"They have weapons we don't. Find the frequencies of the Temp Base. I want to contact them if we see that signal again," Karamazov directed.

CHAPTER 21

RUIN AND REINDEER

Even through the storm, the sky was becoming brighter as Thompson said, "It's daylight, Captain Hogg. We need to do something."

"I don't have any contacts," Mitchel offered.

"How's Reynolds?" Hogg asked.

"Better, Doc. Says. Temperature down, but not back yet," Mitchel related.

"What are our potential targets?" Hogg questioned.

"There are hundreds of miles of mostly mountains south of us. There is a string of airbases used to ferry planes from the US that were built during World War II. Markovo has about 600 people, mostly reindeer herders. That's a significant enough location that even our pipsqueak bomb would be noticed," Thompson related.

"I know those people. All they ever wanted was to be left alone. You are going to kill 600 of them and thousands of reindeer who never hurt anyone. For what?" Petrov questioned.

"I understand what you are saying. That is the least populated area we can hit that we are sure would be noticed," Thompson explained.

"To live, serve the party, procreate, and die. That is what a good Russian is supposed to do," Petrov responded.

"What does that mean?" Hogg demanded.

"He who kills the innocent will die the damned. Those people did nothing. Nothing to disserve what we are about to do to them," Petrov argued.

"Those are our orders," Hogg replied with a firm voice as he was becoming irritated with Petrov's moral dilemma.

"That's what the Nazis said at Nuremburg," Petrov retorted.

"We must kill hundreds to perhaps save millions. You agreed. I heard you. I don't have time for this. We'll discuss these ethical issues later. Now I need you to do what you said you would do to help us get out of here," Hogg replied.

"I did. And now I must die with it," Petrov acquiesced as he put his headphones on to monitor radio traffic.

"Swain, take us up to 35,000 feet. Thompson, prepare the device. Launch as soon as we reach altitude," Hogg ordered.

******

In the tower at Yakutsk Airport, the crew had been increased to four. Lieutenant Voleov looked at the radar screen while Starshina Ivanov unloaded a bag containing bread, sausage, and cheese.

"That strange signal that we were tracking last night is back again. It's 300 kilometers southeast of where it was," Ivanov reported to the Lieutenant.

"Ivanov, you have been here longer than anyone. Have you ever seen anything like this?" Voleov questioned.

"No. I have not. They would see it better from Tiksi or Pevek, I think," Ivanov replied.

"It's not sending any aircraft identification signals. Maybe it is a weather balloon with its radio blown away," Karamazov speculated.

"The Americans fired on our bases. This may be some American weapon. Notify the interceptors at Tiksi," Voleov ordered.

"Lieutenant. The lines are down, and the radio is useless in this storm. We can see, but we can't speak," Karamazov informed as he put down the telephone receiver.

"Did any jets from Temp make it here?" Voleov asked.

"One did," Karamazov replied.

"Ask the pilot to come up. Whatever is going on, they need to know about it in Tiksi," Voleov requested.

"Comrade Major," Volkov began as soon as Major Virch Bradlo entered the room dressed in his fight suit and fur cap that bore his insignia on its turned-up flap. "All our communications are down. The Temp Airbase has been attacked. We can sometimes see a signal we can't identify. Can you take a look with your fighter?"

"I need fuel," Bradlo stated as he had been literally running on fumes when he had searched this leg of the Starburst deployment.

"We don't get jets here. All I've got is 10,000 kilos for helicopters, diesel, and gas for cars and light aircraft," Volkov replied, wondering how soon the ice would allow another fuel barge to reach him.

"Do you have vodka?" Bradlo queried.

"For fuel or for drinking?" Volkov asked inquisitively.

"For both. Mix 20 liters with the jet fuel when you refuel my plane. There is no time to waste. Write me up a document that I requisitioned this fuel to fly a vital mission related to state security," Bradlo dictated.

"I'll have your plane pulled into a hanger and see about your fuel. While we wait, bring your navigator up so he can see what we are observing. After your experiences today, I suspect that you could use something to eat and a drink too," Volkov offered.

"Me, Lieutenant Yakov, and the plane. We're all thirsty. Just a little for us, though," Bradlo requested.

When the vodka and two sack lunches arrived, the men stood and faced a large Russian Federation Flag nailed to one wall in a lower room of the tower.

"Glory to the Russian Federation," Major Bradlo toasted as they all raised their glasses and downed the vodka. After the drink and food, he requested that he be left alone to sleep as much as he could while the plane was being prepared for flight.

******

In Buzzard 1, Thompson stated, "I'm ready to launch."

"Launch the weapon," Hogg ordered.

"Weapon launched," Thompson stated, which was followed a few minutes later by "Confirmed on track. Successful launch confirmed." He could visualize the bomb with its wings and stabilizers extended, flying through the snowstorm, being pushed by a trail of yellow flame as the solid propellent relentlessly drove the bomb towards its target.

"Mitchel, send the Weapon Deployed Signal, and then shut down active com." Hogg directed.

"It's done. God help us all," Petrov said as he fingered his mother's cross around his neck.

"Slade take us down. We're too exposed up here," Hogg said while he unbuckled so that he could address the entire crew face-to-face.

"What course?" Mitchel asked.

"I'm going back to try to talk to Reynolds. Take us northwest for now. We want to keep away from their bases. We don't know what they've got up here – particularly mobile launchers that might be anywhere," Hogg directed.

******

In Pentagon conference room 67, which was filled with men and women in service uniforms looking at monitors as Secretary Hendricks and General Campbell nervously watched the unfolding situation.

"Sir. The weapon is deployed. It will strike somewhere in Siberia in a few minutes. You should be able to see it on this screen. We have a satellite that will provide real-time photos," Campbell told Secretary Hendricks.

"Where are the others?" Hendricks asked.

"One of the B-52s is in Sicily, and the other is at Diego Garcia. They've had problems with the new engines and are working on them," Campbell related.

"Hopefully, they will not be needed. Keep me posted on their status. President Laurence has some calls to make," Hendricks concluded.

******

At Diego Garcia, Louella's crew was in the Ready Room when Base Commander Lee handed Anderson a sealed plastic bag containing documents, which he opened, read, and summarized for his crew. "The situation is that Buzzard 1 has dropped its bomb on a Russian target. We are to stand ready to go in through Pakistan, Afghanistan, and then into Russia to strike somewhere in Southern Siberia," Anderson informed.

"They may be as likely to shoot us down as the Russians," Massauro worried.

"We may have to take our chances. I've sent Washington my ideas, and the diplomats will have to work them out," Anderson responded.

******

The crew from Betty Buster was assembled in the situation room at Sigonella as Collins read his orders and announced, "Gentlemen, we wait. In the meantime, parts are being placed in Betty Buster's engines, and we are to plan an attack through Ukraine."

"What's happening?" Wei asked with an obvious look of concern on his face.

"A bomb has been dropped in Siberia, and negotiations are underway. If they fail, we will go in with our bunker-buster hydrogen bomb that will seal up any underground installations, if not destroy them," Collins related.

"What happened to the crew? Did they make it out of Russia?" Wei asked.

"I have not heard otherwise, so I would suppose they are all right. I'm sorry, but we may not know until this thing is all over," Collins stated with a somber note.

"Any news about Boss?" We really need him back," Brezny inquired.

"Nothing yet. If we are lucky, he will bring the crew and that tanker here. We really need him. I have requested this through channels, but in this confused situation, I don't know if anyone is even reading incoming com. I hope so," Collins said as he clasped his hands together to make a symbolic tent with his fingers.

******

In the Yakutsk tower, Yakov looked in horror as he could see the streak of a missile leave the blob they had been tracking and fly south deeper into Siberia. "Vot der 'mo," he shouted as this unmistakable sign of aggression proved that this blob was no flight of birds or fluke of the storm.

The approaching roar of distant thunder was heard before the people of Markovo turned to witness a blinding flash and obliteration. Herders who happened to be on nearby mountains saw the flash and witnessed the mushroom cloud climb thousands of feet into the sky. In a panic, the reindeer ran. Their crowns of antlers sometimes became entangled as burning debris rained from the sky. The incandescent particles mixed with the charred remains of former lives covered the ground with a dirty black layer mixed with glass particles. Those that survived had run towards water and immersed themselves, seeking to protect skin and fur from the burning particles. Bear, tigers, and wolves that were deep in their dins with their young remained relatively safe, ready to emerge and feed on the dead and dying.

******

Six pair of Mig-31 pilots and navigators were assembled in the ready room at the Anadry-Ugolny Air Force base while the snowstorm raged outside. Colonel Karimoskovsky stood on a podium addressing the crews, "The Americans have attacked us. Our new radar is inoperable, the amount of anti-icing compound we have is limited, and we do not have time to clear the runway. You are to launch as soon as a plow clears a lane. Low altitude icing is expected. If you get into trouble, move your aircraft off the runway or eject. You are to immediately fire on any non-Russian targets. We will continue to clear the runway so that you may return. Aircraft losses are expected. For the Motherland," he concluded as he saluted the crewmen who returned the salute with a unified shout of "For the Motherland."

Launched out of its bunker, the first MiG-31 started its takeoff, and only 20 meters down the runway, the aircraft spun, and its tail struck a parked plane and exploded into a ball of yellow flame.

The second MiG made it past the wreckage of the first, but its engine sputtered, and the MiG was driven into a snowbank.

The pilot of MiG number three attempted to fire its afterburners almost as soon as it started moving, bounced into a snowbank, and started spinning until the pilot killed the engine.

With the runway somewhat better illuminated by burning aircraft, the fourth MiG began its run, the pilot held the aircraft on the runway, fired its afterburner, and made a steep vertical climb.

"MiG 647 to tower. Two thousand feet and climbing. Aircraft acting normally," Pilot Captain Val Ukaroff reported.

"Circle base at 40,000 feet. Activate radar and advise," Karimoskovsky ordered.

Ukaroff keyed his mic to speak with Lieutenant Alexander. "Start your radar and search at maximum range. You are the eyes of Russia right now."

"I have something at maximum scan. It's diffused. I've never seen anything like it. It's slow. Maybe 300 kilometers an hour," Alexander reported.

"MiG 647 to tower. We have an unknown contact beyond our weapon range that is approaching from the southwest," Ukaroff reported.

"If it continues to approach and does not respond to challenge, shoot it down. Remain on station and report," Karimoskovsky ordered.

Turning to the tower manager, Captain Weavisloskev, he said, "I don't want to take any chances with whatever that is. Keep working on the runway, and get two more MiG-31s ready with anti-aircraft rockets, cannon, and full fuel. If that is some American plane, I want it. Or I want it shot down."

CHAPTER 22
FLY OR DIE

Not long after Buzzard, I had been hit with the shock wave of the explosion, Mitchell reported to Hogg, "Sir. We are being scanned."

"Slade have Thompson relieve you. Ready the DDFRs, and take out that radar," Hogg directed.

"That'll take 15 minutes," Thompson replied.

"Hurry, man. If they can see us, they can shoot us," Hogg urged.

******

On the navigator's screen of MiG 647, Lieutenant Alexander saw a rapidly moving object approaching them and told Ukaroff, "Sir. We are being fired on."

"MiG 647 to tower. We have been targeted. Returning fire. Will activate decoys," Ukaroff out.

"Shall I deploy the decoys now?" Alexander asked.

"No. It's too far. Wait," Ukaroff responded.

"Remain on station. Take defensive action as necessary. I'm sending help," Karimoskovsky informed the pilot.

In the hanger a work crew frantically brushed snow and pounded ice off the control surfaces and air intake of MiG 433. After Pilot Lieutenant Helina Bancroff worked the flaps and rudder to make sure they were free, she rolled the MiG down the runway, activated the afterburner, and took off. The MiG flew left, then right, curved over at the top of its arc, and the pilot and navigator ejected to watch their MiG crash below.

******

At the Anadyr-Ogolny Joint Operations Center, a corporal rushed in with a transistor radio in his hands, "Comrade General. The American President is on the radio."

"Give me that radio," Karimoskovsky ordered and put the receiver to his ear to listen. After a moment, he decided, "Put this on the interior speakers."

"People of the Russian Federation. Our two great nations have been engaged in a war in Ukraine, which has resulted in the exchange of increasingly powerful nuclear weapons on each other's territories. An hour ago, a low-yield device was dropped on an isolated Siberian village to demonstrate that the United States has the ability to strike anywhere within the Russian Federation, with the knowledge that the Russian Federation has the same capabilities. This exchange of weapons has the logical end that it will accelerate to the point where the entire planet will be uninhabitable, with the loss of billions of lives. We have no demands. We only ask that this exchange of nuclear devices be stopped immediately."

"What do we do?" Weavisloskev asked. "We've lost four MiGs. I've got to get the ice off our last MiG-31 or it will go down too."

"Pull that MiG back into the hanger and de-ice it. Whatever the politicos do or say, we must defend The Motherland," Karimoskovsky declared.

"Yes. I understand," Weavisloskev responded.

"We have twenty of the most advanced aircraft in the world, a fleet in the harbor, and our fate rests in the hands of a green pilot and an obsolete aircraft," Karimoskovsky summarized.

"That is so Comrade General. I will take her up myself," Weavisloskev declared as he ran through the tower, stopping to get his flight suit and helmet.

"Deploy decoys now," Ukaroff ordered as he turned his MiG up and away, but the missile followed the aircraft through its turn and exploded against one of the decoys, pushing fragments into the fighter's port engine, which burst into flames as the MiG-31 went into a flat spin by the time Ukaroff and Alexander ejected.

******

"Thompson swap off with Slade. Activate your laser weapons for independent target acquisition and fire at anything approaching a mile away," Hogg ordered.

During the time that it took for the two to change positions and for Thompson to activate the laser weapons, the Russian missile had nearly closed on Buzzard 1. Almost immediately, a nearby explosion rocked the aircraft, and smoke began to issue from prop engines numbers 4 and 6.

"Captain. We have smoke from Prop engine no. 4 and a fire from number 6. Activating fire extinguisher on number 6," Mitchel shouted.

"We've got to get the hell out of here. Activate Jets," Hogg ordered.

"Starting jets 1,2,3, and 4. Running up to full power," Swain reported.

"I'll take us to Fairbanks. Don't want to get too close to that base at Vladivostok. There are severe icing conditions at low altitudes across the entire Bering Sea," Mitchell suggested.

"Roger. Take us to Fairbanks. Activate recognition signal when we are back in American airspace," Hogg directed.

"We'll be exposed, Sir," Thompson prompted.

"Don't want to get us shot down by our own people. The Russians have SAM batteries down there. We can expect to be fired on. They can reach us 80 miles out," Hogg informed.

"We're not going to make it. Are we?" Thompson asked.

"We've got one more DDFR, and this storm. Keep your toes crossed. Petrov, if you want to pray. Pray. We need all the help we can get," Hogg suggested.

"O Holy Mother, intercede with your blessed Son to protect this crew and Buzzard 1 and bless the souls of the lives we have taken and give them a richer life in your holy city than they have ever known. In your son's name we pray. Amen." Petrov concluded, clutching his mother's cross.

"Amen. Now let's get out of here." Hogg seconded.

******

In the Anadyr-Ugolny hanger, mechanics melted and beat masses of ice from the wings and tail of a MiG as Weavisloskev arrived.

"Is the ship ready?" Weavisloskev asked.

"Sir. This is Storm Petrel. She will fly," Chief Mechanic Valenskevy reported.

"I need an experienced navigator," Weavisloskev announced.

"I'll go. Sir," Valenskevy responded.

"Get suited up. We have work to do," Weavisloskev announced as he walked around the aircraft before climbing aboard.

******

On Buzzard 1 frantic efforts of damage control were taking place.

"Mitchel. How are those engines doing?" Hogg asked.

"Got the fire out on no. 6. Shut engine off. Still losing fuel," Mitchel reported.

"Have Gonzalez suit up and stop that leak," Hogg directed.

In the crew area, Commander Reynolds woke up, groggily looked around, and saw Gonzalez dressing in protective gear before going into the wing. Petrov noticed and told the commander, "We've dropped our bomb and are trying to get out of Russia. Got a fuel leak in the wing. Gonzalez is going in to fix it."

"Get me up front," Reynolds ordered.

Petrov unstrapped Reynolds and helped him sit up. "In a moment, sir. I've got to get Gonzalez started on stopping that leak."

While Reynolds gathered his senses, Petrov held onto Gonzalez's belt when he opened the door and the pressure differential threatened to suck her inside the wing. Once inside and braced against the wing struts, Petrov gave her the tool bags and extra oxygen. When she nodded that everything was inside, Petrov secured the door's hatches and gave her a parting, "Be careful. Love you."

Gonzalez turned on a large battery-powered light and saw smoke clearing ahead of her, and as she moved past engine no.5, she saw fuel pouring from the bottom of the wing.

Returning to Commander Reynolds, Petrov helped him onto the sled, pulled him to the front of the airplane, and walked him to the cockpit.

******

Storm Petrel, now fully crewed, avoided the obstacles on the runway at the Anadyr-Ugolny base, and Weavisloskev reported, "MiG 315 to tower. We're up and proceeding southeast towards the suspected target."

"Congratulations, Sir. Excellent take off," Valenskevy observed.

"All thanks to the hard work that you and your crew did. Look for a slow-moving target southeast of us. Like a flock of birds," Weavisloskev directed.

"I think I've got it, Sir. But it comes and goes. Need to get closer," Valenskevy requested.

"Set course and get ready for Mach 2," Weavisloskev warned.

"Ready, Sir," Valenskevy responded.

Despite being ready for it, the abrupt acceleration to Mach 2 was always a shock to the body, and Weavisloskev felt like he was being beaten with slats in some exotic massage parlor.

******

The Bering Sea Air Defense System had been alerted, and at the control room at the Anadyr Air Force base, there was a screen showing the location of 34 mobile SAM missile defense units. Captain Cheroff observed an intermittent signal from an object approaching from the southeast.

"Activate units 45, 104, 15, and 96. We have been attacked. Fire on any non-identified aircraft approaching your position. Hold fire until signal makes closest approach," Cheroff ordered.

As Lieutenant Barskey examined a green screen in his battery's control van, he hesitated for a moment. "Was this the target that he had been warned about? Was this an American threat or some foreign pilot whose transponder was not working? If I am wrong, I could kill an entire planeload of people? If I am right, I would be a hero."

"Fire one. Fire two. Fire three. Fire four. Fire five. Fire six. Confirm firing and inspect launcher," Barskey ordered.

Private Orenskev donned his winter clothing, stepped outside, and inspected the launch tubes. When he returned, he excitedly reported, "Missles away Sir. Launch tubes are stable."

******

The launch was detected by Buzzard 1, and Thompson warned, "Six missiles approaching. Laser system engaging. Only belly and top lasers firing. Six targets neutralized."

"Welcome back, Sir. You all right?" Hogg asked.

"I'm mentally all right, but physically not so much," Reynolds admitted.

"Slade, Give Commander Reynolds your seat and help him get into it," Hogg directed.

"The rear laser is not working," Slade said after he returned to his instruments.

"Go back and check on it. Petrov, see if Gonzalez has stopped that leak. The Commander and I have some catching up to do," Hogg informed.

******

Petrov heard Gonzalez tapping on the hatch and helped her get out of the wing and retrieve her tools.

******

"I think I fixed no. 5. There is a lot of fuel in the wing that could go up like a bomb. I think we need a load of fire retardant over it," Gonzalez told her lover.

"Go tell Hogg. I'll see what can be done with the laser," Petrov said before he ran down the passage towards the tail-gun position.

******

"Sir, we should be very close. Slow down, or we could hit whatever that is. It is keeping direction and speed. Its altitude is 1000 meters," Valenskevy recommended.

"It is important that we make a visual identification of this aircraft before we fire on it. I am going to get us closer," Weavisloskev informed his navigator.

Weavisloskev took Storm Petrel down below the clouds and saw the huge aircraft silhouetted against a patch of blue sky. Projecting from its tail was a bent rod, which he assumed was some kind of weapon that appeared to have been damaged.

Suddenly, a loud Russian-accented voice reverberated through Reynolds's headphones, which he switched to speakers.

"American aircraft, this is Lieutenant Weavisloskev of The Russian Federation. I have you targeted, and you cannot escape. Surrender, and I will direct you to an airfield," Weavisloskev proposed.

"Give us a little time to discuss your proposal," Reynolds asked.

"You have only minutes before you will be fired on by a missile battery. If you attempt to fire on it or at me, I will blow you out of the sky," Weavisloskev demanded.

Reynolds mouthed to his crew, "Got to buy some time," and then told Weavisloskev, "This is Commander Reynolds. We accept your terms."

"I will fly beneath you to keep our batteries from shooting at you. Increase speed if possible and continue on the present course," Weavisloskev directed.

"When he comes beneath us, we can get him," Slade suggested.

"As long as we are flying towards Alaska, we need to have him there. If he orders us to turn south, we'll shoot him down and take our chances. We can't allow this technology to fall into enemy hands."

"On the engines, we have four props running, three smoking, and the jets are doing fine. Our fuel can get us to Elmendorf south of Fairbanks or Edmonton in Canada – further if we cut the jets," Mitchel surmised.

CHAPTER 23
ESCAPE

In a secure room below the Whitehouse President Laurence, with Secretary of State O'Dell Roberts by his side, was on the Red Telephone talking to Premier Putin, whose comments are being translated by Nancy Herrington and broadcast throughout the room.

"He says, how dare we attack his country. He said that he will obliterate every city in America," Herrington reported.

"Yes, and we will do the same to every city in Russia, and then where will we be? Do you want to destroy the whole world?" Laurence asked probing questions to see if he could understand Putin's motives.

"He said that he would rather die with honor than live in shame. That is what he said, but something is happening in the background. I can catch 'American bomber' but nothing else," Herrington said with a puzzled look on her face.

"There is no honor in bombing everyone back to the Stone Age. If you are known at all, it will be as the person who destroyed the world. You want that?" Laurence pushed.

"Niet…" and then Putin hesitated.

"He said that the cowardly bastards who dropped the bomb have surrendered and will be put on public trial, where they will confess. Commander Reynolds and his crew will be tried and publicly executed in an interesting manner so the entire world can watch," Herrington translated.

"Is that true? Have they got the crew?" Laurence asked.

"Buzzard 1 is dark. The last word we got from them is that the device was dropped. They were not to make contact again until they entered American airspace," Roberts reminded the president.

"What about the two B-52s?" Laurence asked.

"They are having their engines worked on. The one in Sicily is closest to being ready. We are trying to get fly-over permissions for the one in Diego Garcia," Roberts informed.

"Isn't that information likely to be leaked?" Laurence speculated.

"With officials from four countries involved, I think that it would be impossible to keep someone from selling out to the Russians," Roberts affirmed.

"Start the process, but send the B-52 from Diego Garcia to Australia. We'll let the Russians believe that they are going to be attacked from Kazakhstan while we go in from Ukraine," Laurence directed.

"We don't want that technology to fall into Russian hands. We need to destroy that aircraft," Roberts dispassionately told the President.

"You mean kill our own people?" Laurence questioned.

"Exactly. We can send a destruct signal from here. There are five different devices concealed in the plane. They will never know what happened. Compared with whatever Putin has in mind for them, it would be a better end for them all," Roberts asserted.

"Check your firing links and make sure they are up. We'll give them four hours to be detected by Alaskan radar. Then we will destroy Buzzard 1. When it comes time, I will do it myself," Laurence affirmed.

******

Tension was rising in Buzzard 1 as more of Siberia passed under their wings. It was broken when Mitchel announced, "Sir. On this heading, we will be in American airspace in 15 minutes."

"That fucker. I think he is trying to take us home," Reynolds remarked in a sense of astonishment.

"Sir. We are going to fly over a Russian destroyer," Thompson shouted up to the cockpit.

"Lieutenant Weavisloskev, we are complying with your request. Arming to defend against a destroyer. Drop back and protect our rear," Reynolds requested.

"Roger. I believe you Americans say. Do not fire on the destroyer," Weavisloskev responded.

Explosions occurred around Buzzard 1 as the laser weapons and wing rockets took out four missiles, and Weavisloskev hit two from the rear. Following this exchange, Buzzard 1 and Storm Petrel entered American airspace, and Reynolds activated recognition signals.

"You are now our guests. Do you wish to seek asylum in the United States?" Reynolds said.

"I cannot return to Russia, and I will not betray my Motherland," Weavisloskev replied.

"Understood. We will be escorted by American fighters. When we land, follow us," Reynolds directed.

******

At the Whitehouse planning was continuing with Roberts reporting, "President Laurence, the links are solid. We can do it anytime."

Check with Alaska. See if they can tell us anything," Laurence asked.

"What'a know!" Roberts exclaimed. "I mean, they made it, Sir. They actually made it. Buzzard 1 is being escorted by a Russian defector to Elmendorf Air Force Base under a screen of our fighters.

"Thank God. I did not really want to do that," Laurence said with a sigh of relief.

At Elmendorf Buzzard 1 landed, followed by Storm Petrel with two escorting fighters flying ahead. Both aircraft followed a guide vehicle down the runway towards a large hanger and stopped in front of it. They are met by Base Commander Colonel French, who arrived with jeeps of Military Police.

"Welcome home, you guys, that was a remarkable mission," French said as he shook Reynold's hands.

A pistol shot rang out from Storm Petrel. The MPs and crew members rushed to the plane to find a man dead on the ground with a pistol in his hands, with Weavisloskev standing beside him with his hands in the air.

"Starshina Valenskevy was in the Soviet military and later the Russian Federation Air Force all of his life. Because of my actions, he cannot return. He took what he saw as the only honorable action," Weavisloskev explained.

"We understand," Reynolds replied.

"We will bury him with honors alongside his comrades who perished here during World War II, when we were allies. His contribution to peace was no less than theirs," French concluded.

******

At the Whitehouse President Laurence was astonished when he remarked, "We got them back and a defector too?"

"Yes. They are safely on the ground in Alaska. I have been contacted through diplomatic channels that they want the MiG and its pilot returned immediately," Roberts related.

"They are going to kill him," Laurence stated in a manner to imply the near certainty of his statement.

"No. They are going to make him wish he were dead for every day of the rest of his life. If we don't give them back, they say they will continue the nuclear exchange," Roberts concluded.

******

In French's office at Elmendorf, a tense conversation was taking place with Weavisloskev while Petrov interpreted.

"They want you and the MiG back; otherwise, they will drop a thousand nukes on the US and keep it up until we send you back," the base commander told Weavisloskev.

"Notify them that I will return the MiG to Vladivostok as soon as it is able to fly," Weavisloskev answered.

"You don't have a navigator," French stated.

"I won't need one," Weavisloskev replied.

"I'll go with you," Petrov offered.

"If you wish. It will be a very, very, very long flight," Weavisloskev commented with an air of finality.

CHAPTER 24

REUNION

A decade later, at a new exhibit at the Smithsonian Air and Space Museum, one wing of Buzzard 1 was displayed beside the fuselage. The crew of Buzzard 1 and their families gathered in front of the aircraft, preparing for a photo. Swain and Grace had their two teenage children with them. Bruce attended wearing a suit. He was standing behind Reynold's wheelchair when Weavisloskev and Petrov approached with different escorts.

"You're both alive! We were told that you crashed the MiG at sea and died," Reynolds gushed.

"Petrov and I homed in on an American sub, ditched the MiG over the deepest trench in the Pacific, and were rescued. We've been in Witness Protection ever since," Weavisloskev explained.

Petrov walked over and hugged Weavisloskev saying, "I am sorry about Storm Petrel. She was a good airplane. I sent her down with a bottle of vodka. I would like to share one with you."

"I will, but I have been waiting for ten years to see this remarkable aircraft. I never have you know."

Bruce pushed Commander Reynolds to the front of the aircraft, where Reynolds used his cane to point towards the painting of the red-headed Buzzard on his nose. "You know they called the B-36 The Peacemaker..."

The building shook. Looking up through the skylight, they could see three B-52s flying over in a salute to Buzzard 1 and its crew.

At the reception after the tour, Reynolds and Petrov went into a corner. Reynolds asked Petrov, "Did you ever hear of that FSV agent, Sokolov, who said he would hunt you down?"

"He'll wait until maybe my and Gonzalez's daughter gets married and do it then. The woman I was planning to marry, Rina, will probably do the shooting. She shot me once through the shoulder. Now she is an official Hero of the Russian Federation. Or maybe Fatima, who shoots a 60-caliber rifle that can take out a car at half a mile. To be sure, they will get me somehow. Someday. Maybe even today. I am satisfied that I have done what was required of me. I am ready," he concluded.

******

In a nearby hotel Sokolov, Rina, and Fatima were unpacking a diplomatically sealed box containing a long-barreled Mosin-Nagant rifle equipped with a large scope and silencer.

THE END

www.ingramcontent.com/pod-product-compliance
Lightning Source LLC
Chambersburg PA
CBHW020333010826
48970CB00010B/572